I0547173

Monkey-King's Adventure in America

Sui Duan

©2025 Duan Publishing House

ISBN: 979-8-9868667-4-1

Contents

Chapter One: Monkey-King's Decision to Go to America

Background of Our Heroes

It was duly recorded that Sun Wukong, known also as Monkey-King in Chinese literary legends, was born from a stone, which was the result of a divine energy from heaven and earth.

Wukong, in fact, likes being called Monkey-King, and this nickname has become a household name and a well-known English noun. He has many magical powers, such as transforming himself into anything he desires and turning anything into something else at will. He was capable of carrying two mountains on his shoulders and could travel 100,000 miles in a single jumping somersault. If my serious reader wants an exact number, it's 108,000 miles. But most importantly, the defining traits of Monkey-King are his brave fighting spirit against evil and his kind heart to help those in need. His weapon was a golden staff that could extend and shrink freely whenever he wished. When not in use, this golden staff was usually shrunk to the size of a pin and stored in his ear. He could pull his hair from his head, and with a puff, turn these hairs into many copies of himself! These little monkeys then become his helpers. Isn't that amazing?

Wukong, the Monkey King, had a loyal brother, Zhu Baijie, who had an unfortunately snorty mouth and big ears like a pig. We will call him Pigsy here, as everyone likes to call him that. Although he was lazy and always hungry for good food, he still knew some Gongfu, especially using his handy weapon, an Iron Rake. He was not stupid, but he was clumsy, grumpy, and sloppy in everything he did. You cannot say he was one of those with high morals. He was often selfish and sought personal pleasure, but in times of urgency, he was reliably brave and heroic, ready to sacrifice. He was, after all, a common folk with a natural character. He was funny and straightforward. He was so ordinary in thinking that he truly was one of the guys on any street.

It was also recorded that Wukong accompanied the Tang Dynasty Monks on their journey to India[1] to fetch the Buddhist scriptures. He protected the monk from evil harm and made the monk's journey a success. He crossed mountains and rivers, subdued demons and monsters, and endured countless hardships. After going through eighty-one life-and-death trials, he finally reached the Thunder Monastery in the land of Great Happiness. There, he was conferred the title of the Victorious Fighting Sage by the Buddha of the Supreme Paradise. He was deemed invincible and became well known for his bravery and mastery of combat everywhere under heaven.

Now, back in the eastern land of China, Buddhism had flourished. The weather was always favorable, with rain falling on the farmland whenever water was needed. The harvests were abundant, and the people lived in peace and prosperity. The people were honest, and the country became a safe place to live, where no valuables were lost, and doors were left unlatched at night—a place of natural growth and tranquility. Everyone enjoyed a happy life each day.

Arrogant Monkey-King got paranoid

Wukong, having achieved great success and fame, became increasingly self-indulgent. He spent his days wandering, enjoying the mountains and waterfalls, visiting friends, and seeking out Buddhist immortals to talk with. Because he was naturally carefree and unconstrained, he didn't understand or follow the many rules and formalities that governed others' lives. As a result, his actions

---

[1] At the time, the India Subcontinent was considered to be 'the West'. Monkey-King's travel experience includes his trip to the West with Pigsy and two other Tang monks. The trip resulted in a popular Chinese novel, "Travel to the West".

sometimes appeared disrespectful, left people around him puzzled, and made them raise their eyebrows.

Gossip was spreading, and many days went by until one day, the Supreme Buddha called Wukong, the Monkey King to the palace and said,

"Wukong, we know your martial skills are undoubtedly unmatched and renowned, but your literary talents are lacking, and you have no understanding of philosophy, let alone music. Now, the world is at peace, with no demons or monsters to fight, and your talents are of no use. You may return to the Flower-Fruit Mountain where you came from and rest there until we need you again."

Monkey-King wanted to argue, but seeing the joyful faces of the other Buddhas and immortals around, he realized that they were jealous of him. So, he bid farewell to the sacred mountain and, with one somersault, returned to the Flower-Fruit Mountain.

His home return was brisk.

Flower-Fruit Mountain, the Remake of Home

The Flower-Fruit Mountain looked different after all these years. Monkeys of all ages lined up in a two-mile-long formation to welcome their king. Banners fluttered in the breeze, colorful clouds filled the sky, golden light illuminated the road, and horns echoed through the air. Wukong was very pleased and announced,

"Starting today, I will not only focus on practicing martial arts with you, but also study philosophy, music, and every subject, along with the culture of each country, of course. I will write books, give lectures, and boost the pride of our monkeys, while suppressing the arrogance of those Mediocre!"

Monkey-King, always quick to act, immediately got to work. Time passed swiftly; in just a few years, the Flower-Fruit Mountain experienced a total transformation. Today, all the monkeys, both old and young, wear clothes and act in a more refined way. Two hundred-foot-long cloth drapes hung from the cliffs, swaying in the wind, inscribed with sayings, "The sound of wind, rain, and reading fills your ears," and "Philosophy, engineering, and humanities, each one flows from my mouth." Passersby were amazed, and even the birds and animals were impressed by how different the mountains are now.

Monkey-King also introduced new rules at the Water Curtain Cave. Twice a year, the monkeys were evaluated on their progress in learning Gongfu and Literature. Not only did he lead by example, but he also dedicated himself to reading classical texts. He became knowledgeable in everything from astronomy to geography and even published well-cited scholarly works, including 'Analysis of the Temperature of Flame Mountain',[2] 'Investigation of the Water Source of the River of Sand', 'A Record of Customs in the Western Regions', 'The History of Foreign Relations in the Tang Dynasty', 'The Basics of Horse Management',[3] 'The Three Treasures of the True Scriptures', and 'The Theory of Monkeys, Apes, and Humans'.

The list goes on and on.

The Changing of the World

As time passed, Monkey-King dedicated himself to studying. As a result, the moon and sun continued their cycles unnoticed. Then, one day, a small monkey rushed in with urgent news, saying, "The Supreme Buddha has issued a decree that from next month, grain rations will be cut in half, and expenses for all experimental equipment and books are on our own. Medicines must also be paid for by ourselves."

Monkey-King put down his books and asked, "Why is this?"

---

[2] MonkeyKing passed the "Flame Mountain" on his trip to the West.
[3] MonkeyKing was assigned the position of Manager of the Celestial Stable before his trip to the West.

The little monkey replied,

Your Majesty may not be aware of how quickly things are changing. In today's world, anyone can become a Buddha simply by paying a registration fee. People no longer need to take long journeys to seek truth and gain fame, as you once did. Now, there are over a hundred thousand well-known 'gods' and 'monks' who receive stipends in the Buddha system every month.

Monkey-King scratched his head and said, "Why don't you guys print and publish my works? Then use the proceeds to buy grain and supplies. I cannot let my monkeys live on nothing but fruits and vegetables!"

More days passed, and the little monkey came back with more bad news: "There is no grain left in the cave now. We've been publishing your books and selling them all over the world, but despite the hard marketing work and sincere effort, no one is buying them. Only a few copies of 'History of the Tang Dynasty' were sold in Xi'an because of its longstanding cultural heritage. Otherwise, we wouldn't even have enough money for the return trip home. The elders in Xi'an said, 'Buying these books is a way to support Monkey-King, as you once helped the Tang Monk build the capital city of Xi'an.'"

Another little monkey complained, "This year is the Year of the Monkey, but in the capital city, all the calendars are filled with images of beautiful women and celebrities, and no one has even mentioned anything about monkeys. It's infuriating."

Monkey-King, feeling discontent and confused, decided to wander around with his fellow monkeys over the white clouds in the sky. Their group traveled to the Eastern coast, where tall buildings rose, and vehicles moved constantly, creating a bustling scene. A monkey said, "Look, these days, the people are prosperous, but they care more about wealth than culture. They do not read books. Life becomes hard for the scholars."

Monkey-King, Monkey-King, clenched his mouth shut and remained silent as he continued his journey. They soon reached a mountain with dense forests and temples rising one atop another. Many people were carrying goats and cows as sacrifices up the Buddhist mountain. One old monkey said, "This is the sacred place of the Guanyin Bodhisattva, where people give offerings and burn incense to ask for favors to have more children."

Monkey-King was visibly upset and said, "Guanyin, is she interfering with family planning?[4] Is it true that we have one- or two-child policies in place? But how can she receive offerings like that? ..."

"Let's move on, I won't argue with her for Buddha's sake."

As they continued their journey, they came across a massive building that reached the clouds. People stood in long lines, each holding a red envelope and appearing uneasy. Monkey-King landed on the roof of one building and asked, "What is this place?"

A monkey replied, "This is the hall of the Barefoot Immortal, where he practices medicine. The red envelopes are gifts, so they can be admitted to see him. The Barefoot Immortal[5] makes millions every day."

Monkey-King was furious and said, "I've known the Barefoot Immortal for years. He only knows a few weeds in the

---

[4] There was a period when China had a strict policy on the number of children in family planning.
　　[5] Active between the period of 1968-1978 in China, "Bare-Foot Doctor' usually lacked formal medical training, primarily working at the lowest level of the medical system in rural areas.

15

fields and hardly any genuine medicine. He muddles through life as a doctor for some flu symptoms. How dare he sit in such a grand hall and exploit the people? He's not one of us!"

Another monkey explained, "The Barefoot Immortal has been to Japan in the East and recently returned, earning a reputation by calling himself a 'doctor.' People now admire foreign diplomas and flock to him. It's not like the old days when he was just a poor, wandering, obscure medicine healer."

After traveling for a while, they returned to the Flower-Fruit Mountain, but to their surprise, the monkeys were no longer playing or reading. It was eerily quiet, very unlike before. Some older monkeys stumbled forward, saying:

"Your Majesty, King of the mountain, it's terrible! The monkeys are rebelling! They can't stand the hardships of studying here and are seeking adventure elsewhere. Some of them have gone overseas to seek their fortune!

"They left words even saying that your fighting skills are outdated, they may have been valued centuries ago! But not now!"

"They claim that your journey to the West was limited to India and Myanmar, not going west far enough, and that your followers today even become too embarrassed to speak of it."

Monkey-King fell into silence. After a moment, an old monkey sighed, "When we first followed the King to build our empire, we were united and unstoppable; even the Jade Emperor's celestial army couldn't defeat us. Who would have thought that one day we'd be in this situation… money, greed, and fame corrupt people."

Monkey-King asked, "What should we do now?"

The old monkey suggested, "Why don't you study abroad for a year? When you studied with the Buddha in the Indian Subcontinent, you learned the art of transformation, which has benefited you. Why not go somewhere else to earn a foreign diploma? This Flower-Fruit Mountain is fine for now. After you return, this place will have a fresh start and rebirth."

Monkey-King replied, "Sounds like a good idea. To 'read ten thousand books and travel ten thousand miles' is the way of learning. But where should I go?"

The old monkey said, "Don't go to Japan in the East again. The Barefoot Immortal has already made his name there. It wouldn't seem you have ingenuity. You should go far, go to the Western Hemisphere. That's at the edge of the world, the farthest place you can reach."

Monkey-King was overjoyed, saying, "My three somersaults would cover the distance of that trip! I'll leave tomorrow!"

This is how the Chinese would describe Monkey-King's mind: An eagle that hasn't flown in three years, but today it will shatter the sky with just one flap. An eagle that hasn't sounded in nine years will shake the world with a single call today!

The Challenge From North American Elites

As Monkey-King and the monkeys were talking about his exciting upcoming trip, a small monkey from the front gate rushed in with a message.

"The Supreme Buddha summons you!"

Without delay, Monkey-King leapt over a moving cloud and rushed to the Thunderclap Monastery.

Inside, the Buddha sat in the center, surrounded by an assembly of Bodhisattvas and enlightened beings. After paying his respects, Monkey-King took his seat.

The Buddha spoke, "Wukong, a challenge declaration has arrived from the Western Continent (America) by a group of warriors. They proudly claimed that their once-untamed land is no longer wilderness. After centuries of development, the land of America has flourished through the efforts of courageous warriors and wise scholars who have drawn from the strengths of many other nations. Today, their economy thrives, and their technology has advanced beyond recognition. They claimed to have a superior education system to produce mighty warriors. Among them are many valiant and gifted individuals. They have formed the so-called Ivy League Battle Alliance, headed by Master Restivo. They wish to test their might against the greatest heroes of the Eastern land of China. They boasted their cultural superiority and drafted universal principles that everyone agreed to follow if they were defeated."

"Years ago, when I sent you away, I already predicted this very moment. I know that through years of diligent study, you have become skilled in many ways, and your words carry wisdom as well. All these are in addition to your old magic fighting power. Why not accept this challenge? It would not be in vain for all the effort I have put into you!"

Monkey-King laughed, "Many sitting in this hall are learned and dedicated, studying day and night. Why not let them take the challenge?"

The assembled Buddhas quickly stepped back with a humbled response, "We are of humble abilities, only capable of reciting sutras. The journey to America is long and treacherous, separated by vast oceans. Unlike you, the mighty Great Sage, we lack the skills to undertake such a journey. Please have some sympathy for us and entrust this task to yourself!"

Monkey-King then muttered and declared, "If that is the case, then I shall accept this challenge! Let us see what talents those American Elites possess, to speak such bold words!"

The Supreme Buddha then pondered for a moment before speaking again:

"America was known for having warriors and brilliant minds. I heard a lot about this newly formed alliance, the so-called 'Ivy League.' They often look down on others, and whenever they achieve success, they call it a universal truth. If you encounter them, they will likely refuse to yield and demand a contest to prove superiority."

Monkey-King replied:

"I decided to seek understanding of America rather than to triumph over these nameless people. Since I last left you, I have studied scriptures and teachings from various schools of thought. Through this, I've realized that the most challenging, yet most crucial virtue is recognizing your limits and understanding the unknown."

The Buddha was surprised to hear what Wukong said and nodded in approval, "Indeed, the ocean's vastness comes from embracing all rivers; the mountain's greatness lies in accepting every stone and grain of soil. A river does not reject small streams, and therefore, it reaches its depth. Seeing you attain such enlightenment makes me very happy."

"Go, Wukong. Have a nice trip," Buddha continued.

Prepare the Trip for America

Monkey-King returned to the Flower-Fruit Mountain to prepare his trip to America.

"Don't rush," the old monkey warned. "The Western land is one of the Four Great Continents. Unlike two hundred years ago, it's no longer a vast wasteland full of wild buffalo. They built a million iron cars and drove the buffalo away. Now they've become an arrogant nation. They call themselves 'America' and make laws for other countries to follow. If nations don't agree, they resort to force, and they've even built 'Iron Dome' with missiles to patrol their skies. You can't just fly there. It's better to take a more normal route. You need to visit the American embassy and request something called an entry visa. In any case, you'll need to look the part of a proud visitor from a grand nation in the Far East.

Monkey-King agreed and sent a small monkey to the American embassy to handle the visa paperwork.

The next day, the little monkey returned, feeling downcast. "The Americans are too unreasonable. Not only did they refuse to issue the visa, but they also accused Monkey-King of having 'immigration tendencies.' I tried to reason with them, explaining that our master, the King, has special talents unlike any other visa applicant—he can transform into anything he wishes, fly on clouds, and summon the wind and rain. I said the King had no interest in staying in America. But when they heard about the King's ability to move mountains and fill seas, they shut the doors and wouldn't even respond. They claimed that this hearsay couldn't be verified and was superstitious.

Monkey-King was furious and shouted, "How dare they act so rudely! I am the King of Flower-Fruit Mountain, the Great Sage Equal to Heaven! I cannot be treated this way! I'll flood them with the waters of the Three Rivers!"

An old monkey intervened, saying, "Be patient, your majesty, the Americans are very strict and foolish, and they follow strange rules. They don't care for unusual abilities like 'transformation powers' or 'fire-quenching talents.' The little monkey brothers should not have even mentioned those things to foolish Americans. They are too naive to appreciate these magical skills. Let me go and handle it myself."

The next day, after waiting outside the embassy for a long time, the old monkey successfully got the visa. The paperwork was processed swiftly and without a hitch.

Departure to America

Monkey-King, now ready for his journey, waved to the crowd and said, "This adventurous trip to the Western Continent will be interesting. I bet the two cultures will clash. The world is going to see an inevitable confrontation. The tide of the world is immense—those who follow will thrive, and those who resist will perish. I will return with new stories to share with you all."

And with that, the Great Monkey-King dove into the water surrounding the Flower-Fruit Mountain in a big splash. Tall waves rose in the ocean amid cheers and thunderous noise.

Here goes a poem to commemorate Monkey-King's Departure:

> *Deep forests bloom, flowers grace the Eastern Land,*
> *Beneath white clouds, skies so blue, the distant seas expand.*
> *Monkey-King left home and hearth behind,*
> *With a steadfast heart and purpose in mind.*

Ahead surged a mighty tide so grand—

The Western world, America, waited; he'd withstand.

To know what happens in that vast and mysterious land, stay tuned for the next chapter!

Figure 1That day, the little monkey came back feeling sad and reported, "The barbarian officials have gone too far with their bullying. Not only did they refuse to give the papers we needed, but they also accused our Great King of having 'immigration tendencies'!"

Chapter Two: Reunion in Manhattan – Pigsy's Advice

The First Sight

In the western part of America, a sudden golden beam of light shot out from the ground as Monkey-King emerged amidst a big 'Bang'. He then floated atop a cloud, gazing at the tall mountains and endless forests below. Black bears and elk roamed freely, while squirrels and pheasants flitted among the trees. Birds soared through the sky, insects hummed in the underbrush, and beneath the vast blue sky, a lush, fertile land stretched for miles, dotted with grazing cattle, horses, and sheep.

"Truly, a vast and sparsely populated land," Monkey-King sighed. "What a wonderful place. I remember that centuries ago, my homeland, the Tang Empire, also had such breathtaking landscapes. But over generations of farming and neglect, its ecology has degraded to what it is today."

As Monkey-King continued his journey, the roads beneath him crisscrossed like a web, wide and smooth. Countless iron carriages[6] raced alongside each other, roaring past like a tidal wave. He noticed tall green road signs with white lettering on a green background, displaying a foreign script reading "110 miles to New York," alongside a few strange symbols. Perplexed, he looked at an illustration of a knife and fork and guessed it might lead to a training ground, his excitement growing. "Since I've traveled all this way to study, why not meet some American heroes and test my skills? If I encounter a tough fighter, exchanging a few blows would make this trip worthwhile."

---

[6] Automobiles on the road is usually the first amazement for a foreign visitor to find.

Then, noticing male and female symbols on a sign, he chuckled. "I've heard that foreigners care little for dress codes. Could it be that they openly advertise their pleasure houses on the road?"

New York City, Everyone Rushing in the Crossroads of the World

In the heart of New York City, Fifth Avenue was lined with skyscrapers reaching for the sky. Monkey-King descended, gazing up at the buildings that towered like the walls of a deep canyon, filling residents with an overwhelming sense of pressure. The streets bustled with hurried pedestrians, their expressions serious and eyes focused ahead, as if unaware of everything around them.

Dear readers, what you see here is the famous 'Rush Hour March' of New York's office workers. It is a phenomenon rarely noticed by outsiders, yet some poetic souls have left behind a well-known verse:

> *Look ahead, but never around, walk your path with haste.*
> *Do not pause, do not turn, walk your path with haste.*
> *Close your lips, speak no words, if elbows clash, so be it.*
> *Say a quick 'sorry' and keep moving along your path.*

Along the avenues, banks and department stores lined the streets, each guarded by burly men in uniform, dressed with fierce expressions, vigilantly watching the bustling crowd. Street vendors were scarce, and those present did not call out to passersby. Though the signs were numerous and dazzling, an unspoken order reigned amidst the chaos. These Americans were truly citizens of a global metropolis, unaffected by the bizarre and unfamiliar. How so? Despite his monkey face and fur-covered body, not a single person paid Monkey-King a second glance!

You must understand, dear readers, that New York's population comes from all over the world. Here, you will meet people of every skin color—black, white, yellow, and red. There are those with slanted eyes and hooked noses, long limbs and short torsos. Their hair is in every color imaginable, and it is often hard to tell what is natural and what is dyed.

Monkey-King was thoroughly amused by the scene when, suddenly, a slender foreigner blocked his path. The man wore an earring in one ear and exuded an air of ambiguity. Noticing Monkey-King's curious glances and aimless wandering, he thrust a few pages of a booklet into Monkey-King's hands. Monkey-King, attempting to refuse, found the man insistent. With no choice but to accept, he thanked him. Yet, the stranger said nothing, swiftly moving on to distribute more pamphlets to others, many of whom recoiled or evaded him.

Glancing down, Monkey-King read the bold black words, "The Universe is Collapsing! The End of the World is Near! Seek Refuge in God!"

He scoffed. "What nonsense! I stand close to the Buddha himself and have heard nothing of such an impending catastrophe. How could this fellow possibly know?"

As noon neared, hunger gnawed at Monkey-King's stomach. Seeing an elderly woman standing by the roadside, he respectfully bowed and asked, "Gracious lady, is there an eatery nearby?"

To his astonishment, the woman turned pale and screamed, "I'm waiting for the bus! I'm waiting for the bus!" She was obviously scared.

Her outburst immediately grabbed attention. Passersby cast wary looks at Monkey-King, mistaking him for a troublemaker. Among them, two men glared intensely, prepared to intervene.

Dear readers, you should know that in America, where crime rates are high, citizens are taught from a young age how to handle potential threats. The first lesson in any self-defense manual is to loudly call for help to attract public attention and thus intimidate potential attackers. How could Monkey-King have anticipated this?

Perplexed by the woman's reaction and the hostile stares of those around him, he felt completely awkward. "I merely asked for directions. Why is she making such a fuss? These foreigners truly lack manners!" Just as he was about to leave in frustration, a familiar voice called out.

"Brother Monkey, wait up!"

Turning around, Monkey-King was stunned. Standing in front of him, dressed in a sharp suit and holding a leather briefcase, was none other than —Pigsy himself!

Surprised Reunion and Pigsy's Story

A verse describes their reunion:

> *Since parting on the journey west,*
>
> *time flows like a fleeting stream.*
>
> *For years, no trace of a brother was seen,*
>
> *yet here, in Manhattan, fate redeems.*

Monkey-King and Pigsy danced with excitement, overjoyed at their unexpected reunion.

After a quick exchange, Monkey-King asked, "Brother, shouldn't you be serving under the Buddha? What are you doing here in America?"

Pigsy sighed, adjusting his tie. "After our journey to the West, the Buddha appointed me as the Cleanse Hall Messenger, which meant overseeing the celestial kitchens with a troop of little monks. It was exhausting, but at least I was always well-fed. Then, times changed. 'Western Winds' started blowing even into our sacred temples. The Supreme Lord filed a petition, claiming that my robust figure was 'unsightly' and 'out of touch with modern trends.' I was dismissed, told to find an academy to further my studies. But those scholarly folks found me crude and unrefined, and refused to accept me. Bah! Who needs them? I, Pigsy, left on my own terms! Whatever will be, will be."

Monkey-King chuckled. "So, times have really changed. But looking at you now, you seem to be doing well."

Pigsy smirked. "After leaving the celestial court, I came to America last year to find some fun. Now, I run a martial arts school in Chinatown, where I teach the Rake skills and welcome travelers from our homeland, tour guides, you know? Just now, I heard someone screaming and thought a bandit was at work—only to find you, Brother Monkey!"

They gave each a high-five.

As they talked, the two walked along and eventually reached a busy plaza. A group of men and women, each holding a sign, marched in a circle, shouting slogans. Still, despite their energy, passersby barely looked at them.

Monkey-King scratched his head. "Their words are foreign to me, but they seem to be protesting against the authorities. Their march is orderly, and they aren't blocking traffic. But tell me, Brother, shouting their lungs out in the shadow of that tall building, how will the officials in the building hear them?"

Pigsy chuckled. "American protests aren't about making officials listen—it's all about getting on TV. The real trick is inviting reporters beforehand if the police come and shove them around, even better! That's headline material. If this were back home, they'd all be taken away in minutes—no more noise, no more trouble."

Fight Gang Crimes In Manhattan

Their conversation led them into an opulent jewelry store. Inside, golden lights bathed the room in a stunning glow. The walls were lined with pink marble, and in the center, a large artificial waterfall flowed down, shimmering in the sunlight. Diamonds, rubies, and emeralds sparkled from glass cases, arranged like a celestial treasure trove. A sharply dressed attendant spotted Pigsy's broad nose and large frame, mistaking him for a wealthy tycoon. Staying close, he eagerly offered assistance, answering every question with great patience.

As they stepped out, Pigsy said, "This district is a haven for the wealthy, but lately, there have been more and more robberies—"

Before he could finish, a deafening explosion shattered the air. A fireball erupted in the distance, causing people to scream and scatter in every direction. Alarms blared, sirens wailed, and amid the chaos, a group of face-masked bandits burst out of the flames. Riding loud motorcycles, their half-black-clad figures revealed tattoos on their arms as they brandished guns and blades. Like a tide of darkness, they charged down the street, mowing down everything in their path.

What a sight to behold! The great Monkey-King wasted no time. In a flash, he leapt into the street and, with a wave of his hand, summoned a mountain barrier, stopping several thugs in their tracks. His voice boomed, "Who are the demons here and dare wreak havoc in broad daylight?!"

The gang leader, unfazed, raised his weapon and fired. Bullets poured down on Monkey-King, but with a flick of his fur, he stayed unscathed, sparks flying off his indestructible body.

The gangsters gasped. Monkey-King laughed. "My steel bones were tempered in Laozi's furnace! Do you think your pathetic toys can harm me? Watch how I deal with you!"

Reaching into his ear, he pulled out a tiny needle and, with a single puff of breath, turned it into his mighty golden stick. With a powerful leap, he soared into the air.

A poem describes the battle like this:

> One in black armor, one in shining gold,
> One fires his bullets, the other wields his golden pole.
>
> One seeks chaos beneath the blazing sun,
> The other brings justice where the streets run.
>
> The black bear rises to howl at the moon,
> The hungry eagle strikes the snake too soon.
>
> The iron bullet charges, swift as the wind,
> Yet his magic strikes faster, none can rescind.

With a feint, Monkey-King struck the gang leader to the ground, sending his minions tumbling into a heap. Terrified, they groveled, begging for mercy. Monkey-King, still furious, raised his staff to finish them off—only for Pigsy to intervene.

"Brother Monkey, don't hurt them too much!"

At Pigsy's shout, Monkey-King hesitated. The gangsters didn't waste any time, scrambling to their feet and hurriedly dragging their injured leader away in a frantic retreat.

"Why stop me?" Monkey-King demanded.

Pigsy sighed. "Brother, you're new here. In America, no matter who you are—old or young, good or evil—everyone has 'equal rights.' If you hurt someone and cause injury, they could sue you. You might be fined a fortune or thrown in jail. And if you end up in prison, I'd have to bring you food! Lawsuits here drag on for years. Even if you win, the legal fees alone could ruin you."

Monkey-King frowned. "I see now. I hear this 'land of freedom' fears not its rulers, but its outlaws. A villain's crimes can be as clear as day, yet the law is tangled in endless red tape, and smooth-tongued lawyers twist truth into lies. Justice here takes decades, if not lifetimes. So, this is true then."

Pigsy nodded. "Even if they're locked up, life inside isn't so bad. Meals are provided, there's air conditioning, and there's a television. Why, just last year, an inmate sued the prison for putting him in a cell with smokers, claiming secondhand smoke hurt his health—and he won! He got a big settlement. A few years later, they let him out, and he went right back to his old ways. Who wouldn't be scared?"

As they spoke, police cars and fire engines raced to the scene. Flames were extinguished with torrents of water, and news reporters hurried in, jostling for the best camera angles, their microphones pointed toward the burning wreckage.

Monkey-King patted his stomach. "I'm starving. Let's find a restaurant."

Pigsy grinned. "Not far from here is Chinatown. Let's eat to our hearts' content."

And so, the two departed, leaving the camera screw puzzled.

Will Monkey-King and Pigsy enjoy their feast in Chinatown? Stay tuned for the next chapter!

Figure 2 As the two of them conversed back and forth, they found themselves, almost without noticing, stepping into a jeweler's shop along the street.

Chapter Three: Opening a Martial Arts School – Pigsy Upholds Tradition, Monkey-King Seeks Innovation

New York City in the 20th Century

It is said: The stars shift, and the wheel of fortune turns. By the end of the 20th century, the great city of New York was falling apart, showing signs of decay. Corruption thrived among officials, laws failed to control the people, and ethics and morality declined daily. The public focused only on personal freedom and pleasure. Families broke apart, hurting children, and schools emphasized "freedom," "choice," and universities were filled with fake degrees, leaving many young men and women with many desires but no job skills. In response to these urgent social problems, caring American scholars and intellectuals, concerned about reality and eager to help people, looked eastward, hoping to find an ancient cure for society. But, before they could analyze cultural differences, waves of immigrants had already arrived from across the land and seas.

Alas, these first-generation immigrants were mainly loyal and brave men from their homelands. Though they left their native soil, they deeply longed for it. Struggling in a foreign land, unable to speak the language and unfamiliar with local customs, they were still highly adaptable. Low-class immigrants worked hard in strenuous labor, took risks without fear, and faced dangers head-on. High-class immigrants, such as professors and scholars, humbled themselves, working tirelessly in laboratories day and night. Strangers in a strange land and unable to find stable ground, they often struggled to find work. Lacking other skills, they turned to cooking and opened restaurants. Soon, the streets of New York were filled with eateries—Chinese and Thai competing fiercely, Vietnamese and Laotian vying for recognition, while Italian and Mexican establishments lined the avenues.

New York, perched by the Atlantic, bustled with merchants and ships during the day, but at night, many places became havens for thieves, forcing good citizens to lock their doors and stay inside. Naturally, the need for self-defense grew, and martial arts schools sprang up. However, these schools varied greatly in quality, with different styles mixing together. Western boxing, while fierce and brutal, relied solely on knocking opponents down with brute force, lacking the agility and evasion of Eastern martial arts. In the streets, ordinary people sought safety rather than combat, making Eastern martial arts widely popular. In recent years, thanks to the rise of martial arts films, martial arts schools gained renewed popularity, though language barriers prevented them from spreading everywhere in NYC. Meanwhile, the animated cartoon characters "Ninja Turtles" had surely captured the Western imagination. They are flipping and fighting ceaselessly on television screens.

Pigsy Runs Marshal Art School

Dear reader, let us return to our story. After Monkey-King defeated the armored bandits on the street that day, he took refuge at Pigsy's martial arts school. The two brothers spent the night reminiscing about old times and catching up on lost years.

Pigsy said, "My mother gave birth to eight of us brothers. Back when I left for the West and never came back, my eldest brother, Dajie, searched the world for me. He also ended up here in America. He worked on transcontinental railroads and then opened restaurants. After building a small fortune, he helped me set up this martial arts school."

Monkey-King sighed, "Brotherhood is no empty promise."

Pigsy continued, "At first, my business was good. But now, running this school has become difficult. Across the street, the Koreans took advantage of my unfamiliarity with the land and opened their own building to teach Taekwondo. They plastered their advertisements all over New York City, and for months, I haven't had any new students while their school is busy with people. It's like they want to put me out of business! My elder brother is so disappointed and worried."

"Could it be that you don't understand the customs of this place?" Monkey-King asked.

"Don't blame me!" These New Yorkers have no eye for actual skill. They don't recognize the power of my Nine-Toothed Rake. That's why Taekwondo is thriving while I remain unnoticed. It's frustrating! If this story reaches China, not just me, your reputation as my friend, Monkey Brother, will suffer as well. I know that land deities everywhere fear you. America should be no different! Why not help me out?" Pigsy complained.

Monkey-King laughed, "That's easy. I'll summon the local land god and have him move that Korean school, the building, and everything else to the Grand Canyon, where no one will find it! Then you'll be the only martial arts school in town, free to thrive."

Monkey-King Summoned Land God

Saying this, Monkey-King called out twice and struck the ground with his golden stick. Suddenly, light burst out, and as the radiance faded, a handsome, powerful Native American man appeared before them.

Worn on his head, bright feathers fair,
A bow and knife hung at his waist with care.
A rugged cloak on shoulders wide was laid,
His copper-red face shone bold and unafraid.

Monkey-King was overjoyed and thought to himself, "What a handsome man! In my journey to China West, I met countless land gods; they all looked weak, cowardly, and cunning. This American guy stands tall, full of righteousness and strength! Perhaps this rich land itself nurtures such great and strong men."

Monkey-King then commanded the man, the local land god, "There are too many martial arts schools in New York. Such establishments require central planning! They cannot simply be opened at will. Centralized planning is necessary for your job! The number of students enrolled should also be regulated. Move all other schools to Colorado and leave only Pigsy's school here in New York!"

The land god replied, "Immortal Sage, you may not be from here, but what you suggest doing is unwise and impossible. In America, we value free competition and equality for all. Businesses thrive or fail based on market demand. Forcing others to shut down is unconstitutional. Furthermore, though this land is vast, every inch is mapped and tracked by satellite with something called a Geographic Information System. Even if I had the power to move mountains and rivers, I could do nothing about the geographic data records."

Pigsy shouted, "You ungrateful little land god! My brother is the Great Sage Equal to Heaven! Even the Jade Emperor respects him! How dare you refuse him?"

The land god retorted, "We Native Americans do not submit to tyranny. It is well known among us, 'Better to die standing than live kneeling.' Your business is in decline, yet instead of improving your skills, you resort to trickery? That is not the way of a real man."

Pigsy fumed, "If I'm not a real man, what am I then? I should teach you a lesson for being disrespectful!"

Monkey-King quickly intervened, "You, Earth Deity, speak well and with spirit. You have a point. I see now. Your land management is difficult to mess around with. In my homeland, lands and mountains are in a tangled account, an uncertain chaos, constantly shifting under bureaucratic whims. No one knows how many mountains there are, nor how much land there is. Here, land is precise and mapped to the inch. There, when encountering high-ranking officials, local officers bow and scrape, unlike you, a bold and upright Earth Deity. Very well, I will investigate the rival school across the street tomorrow before making further plans. You may withdraw for now; when I need you, I shall summon you again!"

Monkey-King's Discovery

The next day, as the sun rose high in the sky, Monkey-King disguised himself as a Westerner and entered the Korean Martial Arts Hall. Looking around, he saw that the training hall was grand and spotless, with hardwood floors covered by leather mats. Cool air circulated, making the environment especially refreshing.

A Caucasian American man, dignified and smiling, stepped forward to shake hands. He introduced himself as the new master of the hall, having studied at Harvard, an Ivy League school, and called himself Adam. Monkey-King was taken aback and thought to himself, "What a small world! I was planning to seek out an Ivy League school, and here I ran into one of its grads. Well then, let's see how his school operates."

Now, dear readers, pay close attention: The US has a group of schools called the Ivy League, and Harvard is one of them. Adam was no ordinary man. Having trained for years, he was well-versed in Greek classics and had also studied Eastern traditions. Because his father fled during the Korean War, he had a deep connection to the Korean Peninsula. From a young age, he trained in Taekwondo.

Upon hearing that Pigsy had recently opened the "Eight Precepts Rake Oriental Martial Hall" in Manhattan, he set up a competing school across the street, aiming to showcase his Brown prowess.

This Harvard elite, full of spirit and arrogance, boasted, "Our Taekwondo martial arts hall is the finest in the Americas, renowned even in the Eastern Continent and the Korean Peninsula. We have passed down our teachings for eight generations and nine lifetimes, upholding a universal philosophy. Unlike those so-called 'Oriental martial halls' with unclear origins, we have the secret guidance of Harvard's founders, who oversee and manage our training." Saying this, he handed Monkey-King a stack of finely printed brochures. Monkey-King carefully examined it; it depicted blue-eyed foreigners striking poses and throwing punches in an earnest manner. Though they imitated martial forms without true mastery, it was still visually appealing. Monkey-King mused, "Recruiting students and spreading one's reputation is crucial. How can one expect disciples to come if they sit idly in an empty hall? This is what Pigsy lacks for sure."

Suddenly, loud shouts erupted as a Taekwondo demonstration reached its peak. Dozens of men and women in martial arts uniforms stepped forward, their waists decorated with colorful belts. They executed synchronized kicks and punches with great accuracy, shouting in unison.

Monkey-King asked, "What do the colored belts signify?"

Adam, clearly pleased, explained with arrogance, "Eastern martial arts are mysteries and require boundless patience to master. There is a long path to learn them, so I have divided them into nine ranks, represented by white, yellow, orange, green, blue, brown, red, purple, and black belts. Beginners wear white, and after three months, they advance to yellow, then continue to progress through exams. Transforming the endless nature of Eastern martial arts into a measurable system is a unique innovation of my Harvard spirit!"

Monkey-King, amazed, thought, "There's some merit to this idea. When I trained under Master Subhuti, I practiced with my staff from sunrise to sunset, year after year, until it became a routine that often felt monotonous. How could these Westerners endure such repetition and tedious days? This system of belt progression offers tangible achievement and motivation in a short time. Perhaps when I revise my book, the *Basic Principles of the Imperial Horse Training*, I should add a chapter on 'Measurable Progress.'"[7]

When Monkey-King returned, he found Pigsy still deeply asleep. Tugging his ear to wake him, he said, "The secret is uncovered; we can act at once. I will give your martial arts school a lift."

Monkey-King's New Trick

Outside the martial arts hall, Monkey-King told Pigsy, "First, let's upgrade this shabby dojo of yours."

He shouted, "Transform!" with a mystical chant.

It was instantly apparent; a towering, majestic martial arts hall emerged from the ground, shining in gold and jade, with winding corridors and soaring eaves. An extensive sign reading "Oriental Martial Hall" gleamed brightly, while cool breezes carried the scent of sandalwood, and air conditioning was hidden within intricately carved beams and painted pillars.

Plucking a few hairs from the back of his head, Monkey-King used a magic puff to turn the hairs into a troupe of small

---

[7] Quantitative control in management was once a new idea in China.

monkeys, each equipped with some kind of instrument — gongs, trumpets, cymbals, and drums, forming a complete brass set. Instantly, a raucous fanfare echoed into the sky, drawing a massive crowd from all over the city.

Meanwhile, Pigsy, now dressed in a deep purple martial robe, energized himself and started wielding his nine-toothed rake with great agility. Silver light flashed as the rake's rings clashed, creating a fierce display. The audience cheered in awe.

Inside the Taekwondo hall across the street, dozens of Western martial artists heard the constant applause from outside. Lacking extensive training, they couldn't resist their curiosity, and they all rushed outside, filling the street with admiration on their faces.

Pigsy, elated, declared, "My iron rake has fought across the five continents and four seas without a match! Even the steel tanks of Russian warlords were gored with nine holes! Your so-called American superman would have no choice but to submit!" The crowd erupted in excitement.

A burly warrior in the audience shouted, "That rake is truly formidable, far more thrilling than Taekwondo!"

Pigsy twirled his rake wildly once more, its silver rings clanging in a whirlwind, obscuring his entire form. The audience gasped in astonishment. After finishing his demonstration, he loudly proclaimed, "This nine-toothed rake has vanquished demons and fought across the land—none can withstand it!" The crowd cheered even louder.

Adam, the elite master of the Korean martial hall, had been observing everything silently. Sighing, he said, "For too long, we were outsiders of this civilization, though I was drawn to Chinese culture and studied at Harvard's Oriental Academy. I have learned to master various weapons and martial techniques, yet I only knew of swords, spears, arrows, and many staffs—never of this formidable rake. Today, witnessing its power is like seeing the clouds part to reveal a bright sky. I wish to discard everything I learned in the past. I hope Master Rake will accept me as his new student." The onlookers eagerly shared his sentiment.

Monkey-King declared, "Accepting disciples is not something to be done lightly!" With that, he somersaulted into the clouds and stood tall against the blue sky and white clouds. Chanting an incantation, he twirled his Golden-Banded stick in the air. Instantly, thunder roared, and lightning flashed as rain poured down, cleansing the world. The crowd cheered, celebrating the divine wonder.

Soon, the rain stopped, and the sun broke through the clouds. A radiant rainbow stretched across the sky. Monkey-King leaped onto the rainbow and transformed his golden stick into golden scissors; he cut the rainbow's long arc into countless sections and threw them to the crowd as sashes to tie around their waists. The people, witnessing such an extraordinary spectacle, were awestruck by the wonders of the universe. Immediately, the city of New York burst into chaos! What a sight! Thousands of people, young and old, began their training with the nine-toothed rake.

Later generations recorded this event in these fine verses:

> *Beyond the mountains, beyond the halls,*
> *Taekwondo and Rake Gongfu compete for all.*
> *Pigsy's Gongfu Hall upholds tradition,*
> *While Monkey-King innovates with a vision.*

To know what happens next, stay tuned for the next chapter!

Figure 3 Pigsy once more whirled his rake in a frenzy, the silver rings clashing with a clang so dense that none could glimpse his form. When at last he drew back and struck a pose, he cried aloud, "Behold my Nine-Toothed Rake, which has subdued demons and crushed monsters, striking across all the realms—north and south, land and sea—none able to withstand it!" At this, the onlookers burst forth in praise.

Chapter Four: Debate on Culinary Culture While Hungry, Steal Peaches After a Full Belly

It is said that proud Pigsy soon became bored after taking on the role of instructor at his martial arts school. He found teaching the iron rake techniques as effortless as slicing tofu. Each day, he demonstrated a few moves with ease, while his disciples diligently trained and made notable progress. Among them, Adam, the Harvard disciple from the previous chapter, was particularly sharp-witted and eager to excel. He was always the first to speak up and take initiative, making it his habit to meddle in every matter. Thanks to Pigsy's careful guidance, he was the first to earn a blue belt. Proud of this achievement, he dubbed himself "Adam, the Deputy Rake Master," a playful nod to his mastery of the Rake Technique, only second to his master, Pigsy.

Pigsy, however, was a naturally lazy soul, hardly diligent in daily training. He also struggled to speak the foreign languages of his overseas disciples, making communication a dull challenge. Therefore, he was more than happy to let 'Adam, the second rake' run the martial arts school. At the same time, he and Monkey-King wandered freely in New York City, seeking adventures, marveling at curiosities, and indulging in carefree wandering. America has a lot for them to see!

One day, Adam, still confident and proud, sensing that the earlier defeated storm had passed, invited Pigsy and Monkey-King to a meal to show off his strength and self-assurance.

"Masters, allow me to host a feast in your honor as a token of my gratitude. I insist that you do not decline," Adam said.

"When it comes to a good meal, your rake master never steps aside. Since you're treating me, how could I possibly refuse?" Pigsy responded with delight.

"It's well past noon, and I was just thinking of finding a nice restaurant to reward my dear brother Pigsy for these days of hard work," Monkey-King added, barely finishing his sentence before Pigsy was already out the door. Pigsy cannot resist any food temptation.

The Streets of Chinatown, New York

On the busy streets of New York's Chinatown, Adam assumed the posture of a seasoned host and declared, "Among the Four Great Continents, New York stands as the ultimate gathering place for global cuisine. Here, one can find not only the finest Western steaks but also the most exquisite Eastern delicacies. Food is a culture in itself and must not be taken lightly. We must seek only the finest to partake." While he was talking, there appeared the typical prideful Anglo-Saxon smile on his face. He surely thought he would teach Monkey-King and Pigsy a lesson about food culture.

Monkey-King responded, "Why did you say that? As Confucius said, 'Let there be no excess in food preparation, nor shall minced meat be too finely cut.' Our Chinese culinary heritage spans thousands of years, blessed by a vast and rich land. We have tasted every bird in the sky, every animal on land, and every herb and fruit that nature provides. In terms of color, aroma, flavor, and presentation, our cuisine has reached the highest level of refinement. No foreign dish from another continent can compare."

"In Eastern culinary traditions, every dish must come with a story, a grand narrative from centuries past. That, I admit, is something Western cuisine cannot match. However, if we examine the deeper moral significance of these traditions, they may not all be

45

as admirable as they seem. Let's put this to the test. Why don't we explore and experience it ourselves?" Adam proposed.

Live Fish Cooking

As they strolled along, Monkey-King pointed toward a restaurant. The others followed his gaze and saw a water tank just inside the entrance, where several live fish swam gracefully. Monkey-King said, "In the southern lands of China, where it is rich in fish and rice, there exists a tradition of 'live seafood.' Expert chefs select the freshest catch, enhance it with the finest spices, and prepare dishes renowned worldwide for their exquisite taste. Don't you think so?"

Adam scoffed, "All these for the amusement of a mere moment, a live fish is swiftly gutted and deep-fried, still gasping as it is served to the table—isn't this alone merciless? Worse still, I have heard of chefs placing live fish in cold water, gradually raising the temperature. When the fish, unable to bear the heat, gasps for air at the surface, the cook stuffs its mouth with spices and continues the process repeatedly until the fish meets its end. Just for the sake of a meal, must we subject live creatures to such torment? This, my dear friends, pains my heart! It is a tradition best left unmentioned."

Seeing Monkey-King go silent for a moment, Pigsy chimed in, "Enough! If we start overthinking everything, how will I ever eat fish again? Let's find another place!" They passed the fish tank window.

The Scent of Roasted Dock

They continued down the street. Suddenly, the rich aroma of roasted meat filled the air, making their mouths water. Following the scent, they saw a restaurant window displaying several plump ducks, golden brown and glistening with oil. Inside, chefs bustled about, sweat pouring down their brows. A large black plaque with gold lettering hung above the door, "Beijing Roast Duck." Below it, a smaller inscription in delicate calligraphy was hard to read—perhaps "Authentic 300 Years Old Brand," or "True Computer-Controlled Roasting," or "Roasted Using Fruit Tree Only"—but its meaning remained unclear.

Monkey-King observed, "In the northern plains of China, where pastures stretch endlessly, livestock is abundant, and the art of smoking and roasting has been perfected. This century-old Beijing Roast Duck, crisp on the outside and tender inside, rich yet not greasy, is legendary. Surely, this should be a top choice? The best of the best!"

"Not quite," Adam shook his head and countered. "As far as I know, these ducks were raised on farms where the forced-feeding method was used. The force-feeding of ducks has long been debated. The poor birds are confined to small pens, force-fed through tubes inserted down their throats, while machines drive the food into their stomachs. The ducks struggle and shake, but their necks are clamped—there is no escape. Whether or not this violates ethical principles, I shall not discuss. But I have also heard that, to achieve the perfect roast, a hot iron plate is placed beneath the duck's feet. Unable to withstand the heat, the duck lifts its feet, desperately shifting from side to side. Only when its skin thickens and crisps from the heat do the chefs sever its feet and serve them. Alas! How can one bear such cruelty? We wish this had never happened! I fail to understand how anyone can revel in such suffering. It is truly lamentable!

A Question of Culture

Thus, while talking and arguing, the three continued their journey, with Pigsy and Monkey-King silent in thought, and Adam

47

remaining firm in his moral stance. Adam had been winning the debate so far. Amidst the vibrant culinary scene of New York, they faced not only a feast for the senses but also a deep discussion on the ethics of food culture.

Pigsy complained, "I can't eat fish, I can't eat duck—am I supposed to become a vegetarian monk? Yet you Americans devour turkey and beef with delight while preaching kindness and being humane?"

Adam replied, "The food chain spares no one. To eat to grow and then die or become food to be eaten—that is the natural order of all living things. The principle of nature is in eating, but not in how one eats. One should not subject the food creature to unnecessary suffering just for the sake of taste or entertainment. That is to say, being consumed is part of the natural order, but being tortured is not. In our civilization, we avoid cruel cooking methods. Additionally, the United States has strict laws to ensure that livestock and poultry, though raised for food, are not subjected to unnecessary suffering. For example, during transport, animals must be given a rest every seven hours—those who violate these rules face hefty fines."

Monkey-King remarked, "These so-called cruel cooking methods you describe—whether with fish or duck—are mostly hearsay and may not be entirely true. However, in China, people do place great importance on cooking techniques. Often, too much time is spent in the kitchen focusing on elaborate preparations, which is really a shame and a waste of time."

"I, famous Pigsy, don't bother with such formalities and words. I've spent my life struggling to get a full meal. As long as I can eat my fill, that's all that matters. F-K the natural philosophy of eating and drinking." Pigsy chimed in.

48

Adam continued, "Food is a gift from nature, and in America, having three proper meals a day is enough. Yet I have observed that people in China take an opposite approach, considering the pursuit of exotic and unusual foods a marker of social class distinction. Rare birds and wild beasts are turned into delicacies, and those fortunate enough to eat them proudly boast about it, rather than feeling ashamed."

In today's China, wild animals are rarely seen. People should reflect on this reality. It takes time to eliminate longstanding bad habits. They are gradually changing," Monkey-King sighed.

At McDonald's

The group kept walking and soon left Chinatown. Suddenly, they saw a McDonald's by the road. Its red and yellow colors caught the eye, and a big golden 'M' flag was flying alongside the American Stars and Stripes. Seeing this, Adam's face lit up with happiness.

Adam said, "You all see. Hot dogs and cold drinks—nutritionally balanced, clean, and convenient—are popular across all continents, with millions sold daily. This is a great choice! I've even heard that in China, some people hold their wedding banquets at McDonald's—how grand and popular it must be![8]"

Monkey-King scoffed, "Two pieces of bread with a sausage in between—tasteless and bland. It merely serves to fill the stomach. If one were to eat like this every day, what joy would there be in food? It would be no different than attaching a zipper to one's belly—opening it only when necessary to refill. I see that Western industrial culture has infiltrated the food scene, treating people like

---

[8] In the early days, when it was first introduced, McDonald's was a fashion for young people.

machines and reducing meals to mere refueling. Fast food chains mix standardized ingredients to ensure calorie intake, prioritizing efficiency over taste. Consumers are treated like cattle on the farm. Moreover, some industrial giants dislike seeing people eat naturally grown rice and despise them for it. Instead, they grind grains into powder, mix them with artificial flavorings, sugar, and salt in precise proportions, and turn them into colorful cereal flakes for sale. Alas! People have an insatiable appetite—how can they resist such temptations? I lament for Americans who consume industrialized foods and chemically engineered beverages daily. This culture deeply violates the natural order, leading to obesity and countless diseases. Fat, Fat Americans!"

"McDonald's is no good! I, famous Pigsy, ate a bit too much of it the other day and couldn't even take a proper bowel movement and fart well," Pigsy groaned. "Forget their hot dogs and cold drinks. There's a buffet restaurant around the corner. I am hungry. I cannot wait. I'm heading there instead. After walking this long, you two can keep debating. If you find a good place, come and get me." With that, the ever-hungry Pigsy couldn't wait any longer, leaving Monkey-King and Adam to continue their discussion behind.

The All-You-Can-Eat Buffet[9]: A Paradise for the Gluttonous

Dear readers, buffet restaurants are a common sight in America. These establishments are usually spacious, with tables and chairs arranged along the edges. In the center stands a long, waist-high counter that stretches several yards in length and a few feet in width. Two deep trenches are carved into its surface, holding dozens of stainless steel trays filled with a variety of foods. Chefs move back and forth, constantly replenishing the trays with chicken,

---

[9] Buffet restaurant was a new type of eatery to many Chinese people in the 1980s.

vegetables, meat, and fish. Customers are free to take as much as they want, with no restrictions on quantity or type. This setup has never been seen in China. Oh, what joy for food lovers across the land to find in this restaurant setup!

If you ask, "With such an eating style, wouldn't the restaurant suffer losses?"—not at all. The fact is, America is obsessed with dieting. They also hate obesity. They do exercise after eating. They call it 'workout'. They are afraid of gaining weight. They know it is hard to lose it after gaining. They control their eating. Who would dare overeat and bring about their own health downfall? In American offices, obesity is the number one reason to be shamed. However, if this were in China, such a business model wouldn't survive, at least for now.

For Pigsy, however, a buffet was the perfect battlefield—his chance to shine! Here is the poem describing it:

> As soon as he entered,
> his eyes gleamed with excitement.
> He rolled up his sleeves, ready for action.
> As if after five hundred years of hunger,
> His stomach was rumbling with anticipation.
> Today, he could feast to his heart's content!
> As if this is the last meal.
> First, the meat, then the vegetables,
> He piled his plate high, indulging in both the savory and the fresh.
> He ate fish, he ate chicken—he devoured everything,
> May it come from the sea or sky, food, all are alike.
> No questions asked, "Meat not tender? Rice too hot?"—none of that mattered to him.
> In the blink of an eye, he gulped everything down.

He drank soups, he slurped porridges—and he was
finally full,
The time of hunger would never strike again!

A crazy scene! My reader may also like to hear this same poem sung with rhyming below.

As soon as he entered,
his eyes lit up—delight was centered.
He rolled his sleeves with eager might,
prepared to conquer appetite.

Five hundred years of starving rage
had built a hunger hard to cage—
his stomach thundered, wild and bent,
for this, this glorious feast event!
Today he'd dine beyond restraint,
as though this meal were the last meal sent.

First the meats, then greens beside,
he stacked his plate—a tidal tide.
He ate the fish, he tore the chicken,
no matter they out of earth or air—no pickin'.
From sea or sky, all foods were kin,
each morsel gladly welcomed in.

No fuss of "meat too tough" or "soup too hot,"
such petty thoughts? He had them not.
In barely seconds—swift and sure—
he cleared his plate, down to the core.

He drank his soups, he slurped his grains,
till fullness coursed through all his veins—
and hunger's shadow, lean and grim,
could never dare return to him!

Pigsy's Buffet Battle: The Aftermath

Inside the restaurant, the waitstaff watched in astonishment as Pigsy devoured the food like a storm sweeping across the land. Everything in the storm's path was gone. One server hurried to inform the manager, "There is a pig-mouthed customer outside who has eaten a staggering amount of food without pausing for even a moment! I have already set out a three-day supply, yet he continues. What should we do?"

The restaurant owner replied, "A buffet exists so that guests may eat all they can—that is the rule of my establishment! Don't bother to ask. Do your job and stop worrying. Just keep refilling the trays. Why? Do you think he has a bottomless stomach? No way!"

However, recognizing how serious the situation was, the owner quickly called in the backup evening staff. They lined up in a long line, passing dishes in a steady flow to restock the buffet.

Meanwhile, Pigsy, overjoyed and oblivious, kept on his feast as if this were the final meal of his life and there was no tomorrow. Between bites, he muttered to himself, "All this talk about balanced nutrition and calorie limits—it's nonsense for the retarded, and I am worry-free! Those who preach such things are just starving ghosts tormenting themselves."

Seeing the overwhelmed kitchen staff struggling to keep up, Pigsy waved them off and declared, "Why trouble yourselves? Just tell me where the food is stored, and I'll help myself." With that, he wobbled into the kitchen, knocking everything off the stoves, out of the trays, and even from the storage racks onto the floor and into his mouth.

The onlookers, witnessing this legendary glutton, either stared in shock or stifled laughter behind their hands. Some waiters secretly started estimating that today's tip could be sizable.

After stuffing himself to his heart's content, Pigsy felt sleepiness creeping in. He shook his sleeves, preparing to leave. However, as he reached the exit, he suddenly turned back, spotted two large peaches, and stuffed them into his robe.

Hmph! I'll take these back for Monkey-King Brother to try. That monkey is probably still starving, talking nonsense about the 'Tao of Eating' to that stupid idiot Adam.

The Great Buffet Brawl

At this moment, the chefs and staff, who had already been grumbling, suddenly flew into a rage!

You see why? The buffet restaurant had a strict rule: you could eat as much as you wanted inside, but taking food outside was strictly forbidden.

Not only had this pig-mouthed glutton eaten to excess and left without tipping, but now he was stuffing food into his robe to take with him!

How could they let him get away with this? Just consider the tips they've lost from their services!

With a valid reason to act, the whole staff moved quickly and took Pigsy to the ground, binding him securely.

At this point, Pigsy, now full and sleepy, was too slow to react. His belly jutted out, his eyes drooped, and his martial skills—if he still had any—had long since faded.

All he could do was curse loudly, but it was too late—who would've thought that after all his heroic exploits, he'd end up captured in some obscure American buffet restaurant?

What will become of Pigsy? How will he escape this culinary catastrophe?

To find out, stay tuned for the next installment!

Figure 4 The party soon left Chinatown and came across a roadside McDonald's, its red and yellow colors shining brightly. Above it, the golden "M" waved side by side with the American flag. Seeing this, Adam's face lit up with joy.

Chapter Five: Disputes Brought to Court – Monkey-King Brings in Grand Finale

At the buffet restaurant, Pigsy was tied up in the corner, struggling to stand but unable to do so. His mouth had been sealed shut with tape, keeping him from cursing. The kitchen staff gathered to discuss what to do with him when suddenly—CRASH!

With a loud 'Bang', Monkey-King smashed through the window!

"Wild scoundrels! How dare you abduct my brother? I'll beat your souls out of your bodies!" Monkey-King roared.

The restaurant staff stood frozen in shock. A few brave ones rushed forward to block Monkey-King's path, but before they could react, they were knocked to the floor by a few quick blows from Monkey-King's golden stick. Others, emboldened by their numbers, grabbed chairs, brooms, and whatever else they could find to fight back.

Instantly, chaos broke out. Plates and bowls flew, tables flipped, and the sounds of breaking glass and crashing furniture filled the restaurant. The diners screamed and scattered in all directions.

Realizing the fight was getting out of HAND, Monkey-King tucked away his stick and shifted to hand-to-hand combat, launching a flurry of martial arts moves. His movements were unpredictable—striking east but attacking west, feinting north only to hit south. At one moment, he soared into the air, executing a Twin-Wind Palm strike. Next, he rolled across the ground, delivering a precise Immortal's Leg sweep. His techniques, White Crane Spreads Wings and Golden Monkey Steals the Moon, dazzled the crowd.

Outside the restaurant, Adam had been watching the spectacle unfold. Eyes wide with amazement, he clapped and cheered, "What a monkey! What a monkey!" The onlookers are excited to gather around to watch the world-class Gongfu fight.

Pigsy Joins the Fight

Meanwhile, Pigsy in the kitchen corner, as if waking from a dream, suddenly let out a furious roar, snapped his binding ropes, and grabbed his iron rake, swinging it wildly. Walls cracked, pillars toppled, and the entire restaurant was thrown into chaos. Seeing that they were no match for the two warriors, the kitchen staff screamed in terror and fled. The restaurant owner, unable to escape, was lifted into the air by Pigsy and thrown onto the buffet table—accidentally triggering the store's security alarm.

Suddenly—WEE-WOO! WEE-WOO!

The security alarms blared across the restaurant.

Within moments, a stream of police cars zoomed onto the scene from all directions, their sirens rattling the ground. The entire NYC neighborhood erupted into chaos as people rushed out to watch.

Several officers jumped out of the police cars—broad-shouldered, square-jawed, and stiff-faced.

The lead officer barked, "Everyone, freeze! Please show me your hands! If you have disputes, go to court! Fighting in public is against the law. All of you—come with us! Let's see how tough you can be behind bars!"

The restaurant staff, shaken and speechless, obediently surrendered, standing meekly along the wall. Monkey-King, however, smirked to himself. "I, the Great Sage, have never abided by laws. I defied the Jade Emperor and stormed the heavens—what rules have ever bound me?" He mused, "Rather than let these foreign judges meddle with my affairs and tarnish my name, perhaps it's best to make a quick exit. Going back to my home."

Just as he was about to leap into his somersault, which would carry him into a cloud and escape, Adam hurried to his side and whispered, "Defying the police is the number one forbidden act here in America. No respectable citizen likes to defy them. If you run away, won't it show fear in you? Your reputation is on the line."

Monkey-King scoffed, "Nonsense. I have already attained true enlightenment from Paradise. I transcend the cycle of life and death. Why should I fear any law?"

Adam smirked. "I've often heard that people from China don't like to go to court, preferring to settle disputes privately rather than openly through the judicial system. Even Chinese immigrants in America often still keep this old habit. You are brave, Monkey-King. You are different. I was just teasing you, saying you're about to run," Adam chuckled.

Monkey-King raised his eyebrows and declared, "Then today, I shall break this old habit and fight this case in court—not for victory or defeat, but to prove a point!"

Pigsy snorted angrily, "Afraid of a lawsuit? Ridiculous! I did nothing wrong, yet these scoundrels tied me up! My arms are still sore—I demand justice! Let the court judge me, if it is not unfair, I'll beat him until they all roll on the ground!"

A police officer, overhearing Pigsy's loud complaints but not understanding a word of what he said, sternly reminded the group, "Before we proceed, you all have the right to remain silent. Don't say I have not warned you! All your words will be used in court against you."

With that, he escorted them into the police cars.

Adam's Hidden Agenda

Now, dear readers, you might wonder: why was Adam so eager to push Monkey-King and his Pigsy into the legal system? The answer is simple—America's judicial process is notoriously complicated, dragging on for years with no resolution, leaving everyone exhausted and miserable. Although promoted as transparent, the system exposes every private detail in newspapers, on TV, and across the internet. Everything about you would become public. Unless absolutely necessary, no one would willingly get involved in such a legal mess, risking their fortune and reputation.

My dear reader might like to guess another dark secret of Adam: he enjoyed watching Monkey-King and Pigsy in jail and having the legal system push them helplessly down. Then Adam would be the proud winner! He, of course, would not admit this motive to a Monkey and a Pig!

Adam also had his own plans. He knew the media thrived on sensational stories. If they got hold of Pigsy's story, they would love to craft tales from Pigsy's past and turn them into eye-catching headlines like "Pigsy Flirts with Lady Chang-Er" or "Pigsy's Marriage at Gao Village." The public would go wild! Monkey-King and Pigsy, unfamiliar with the American legal system, would be at a disadvantage. Once they lost the case, Adam's legal expertise would be evident, showcasing his proper skills and making him the focus of the news and a hero in North America.

Thus, Adam was determined to trap Pigsy in an American lawsuit, forcing Monkey-King to stay and fight a legal battle he couldn't win, ensuring their scandalous story spread far and wide!

Entering the Court

Soon, several police cars escorted the group to court. Immediately, a swarm of newsmen swarmed in as well. No one wants to miss the chance to report on the warriors from the faraway East of the world.

As they entered the courthouse, Monkey-King observed his surroundings. Unlike the grand, imposing Chinese courts, this place felt more like a bank or a post office, with people casually walking in and out without fear. People just come and go with their disputes, just like visiting a market. Monkey-King found this amusing, thinking, "Perhaps the People of the Americas do not inherently understand right from wrong. Otherwise, why do they require laws to guide them on how to conduct themselves in daily life? Only with laws, they then distinguish between justice and injustice, so everything, big or small, must be judged in court. I, on the other hand, from my inner conscience, recognize good and evil through spiritual insight. Why would I need laws to teach me?"

Pigsy, standing beside him, sighed, "Such a large court and big place, but no public display of criminals, no criticism or rallying cries! Where are the political banners and revolution slogans? It seems there's no public trial today—what a shame, not much excitement."

Noticing their puzzled expressions, Adam explained, "America has been a nation of laws for 200 years. Here, people value personal freedom. Anything not explicitly forbidden by law is permitted. That's why the legal system is so detailed and complex — it's beyond your imagination. In contrast, China has been ruled by emperors for millennia. The people obey and respect the political power above all else, and anything not explicitly allowed by the government is forbidden. It's an opposite system. This is a rare opportunity — why not take this chance to study American law? You may find it enlightening." He smirked smugly as he spoke.

"Every country has its own strengths and reasoning. It can't be simplified into just one comparison—" Monkey-King started, but before he could finish, a group of well-dressed individuals entered the hall. They wore suits and ties, appearing dignified. Each of them held up a sign with prices like "$100/hour," "$1,000/hour," and "$10,000/hour."

Monkey-King and Pigsy were bewildered. "What is this? Are they selling themselves?"

Adam quickly explained, "These are our lawyers—the finest legal minds in America. They graduated from Ivy League Schools. You undoubtedly haven't seen anything like this before."

"It looks more like a slave auction!" Pigsy chuckled.

You're not entirely wrong. For clients, you get what you pay for, "Adam replied. "A $100/hour lawyer has four years of education. They can help you fill out forms accurately and quote legal texts, but lack experience. A $1,000/hour lawyer has ten years of training. They excel in deception, manipulation, and loopholes, though they sometimes slip up. A $10,000/hour lawyer, however, has endured 30 years of legal battles. They can twist facts, revive lost causes, and fabricate stories effortlessly. They are America's best!"

"So, since you also studied at an Ivy League school, you must be in the $10,000/hour category then?" Pigsy asked.

Adam smirked. "We are beyond that. Our skills surpass monetary value—it's a different level entirely."

The Trial Begins

Moments later, a judge in a black robe entered. The room fell silent, and everyone stood up. Once the judge took his seat, he slammed his gavel and announced, "Court is now in session. You must testify truthfully under the Constitution of the United States. Do you all understand?"

Everyone nodded "Yes, your honor" in unison. Pigsy flapped his ears indifferently, murmuring, "The wooden gavel of this court is nothing compared to the majestic wooden block of a Chinese magistrate!" To understand Pigsy, the reader must know that Chinese judges in the old dynasty court used a book-sized wooden board as a hammer to strike the table, which made a loud noise in court. This hammer is called a Threatening Block. Pigsy somehow remembered the old-fashioned court.

Hearing the judges' usual statement, Monkey-King suddenly asked out of nowhere, "In your 200 years of court proceedings, has anyone ever answered 'No' to that question?"

The crowd chuckled.

The judge frowned, "You ignorant monkey! This is a courtroom formality. Just answer 'YES' like everyone else. I'll overlook your impertinence this time since you seem honest and unaccustomed to pretense."

The buffet owner stepped forward and said, "Your Honor, my restaurant was attacked today. Walls were destroyed, ceilings torn open, and I suffered significant losses. Fortunately, two of the offenders were captured. I request justice! I seek compensation."

Pigsy retorted, "These villains kidnapped me! The rope marks are still visible on my arms—examine them closely, Your Honor!"

The judge called Pigsy to the front, examined the marks on him, and then struck his gavel loudly.

The rope marks are clear. Injuries are also apparent. A kidnapping in broad daylight! Clearly, a serious felony. It's a crime that warrants the harshest punishment. Monkey-King, in rescuing his brother, has demonstrated loyalty and courage. The destruction of the restaurant is therefore considered collateral damage.

Seeing the tide turning against him, the restaurant owner hurriedly brought in a lawyer charging $1,000 an hour. The lawyer, a young man, calm and collected, argued, "Mr. Pigsy planned to disrupt the buffet restaurant's normal operations by eating all the food and even trying to take some out. That violated the restaurant's universal rules. The kitchen staff responded to protect their business, though their reaction might have been excessive. Still, if they hadn't acted, future customers might have been encouraged to do the same. The stolen peaches were recovered here as evidence. His theft must have consequences."

He then presented the two peaches to the judge.

The judge immediately ordered the court to produce the record of the amount and variety of food consumed by Pigsy, which totaled three tons and forty-seven different dishes. The judge then banged his gavel again.

Troublemaker Pigsy! You have disrupted public commerce. According to Federal Civil Code §98,765, 'If Pigsy disrupts Buffet Restaurant, he shall be sentenced to three years of community service.'

"Oh, my dear mother!" Pigsy groaned disappointedly.

Monkey-King immediately objected loudly, "The buffet has no restriction on the amount of food a customer may consume. My brother never left the premises, so the charge of 'taking food out' is a false accusation!"

The judge cross-examined the witnesses and confirmed that Pigsy had not yet left the restaurant with the two peaches. He then turned to the restaurant owner and banged his gavel again.

Brazen merchant! How dare you deceive the court and frame Pigsy? According to Federal Civil Code §98,766, 'If Buffet Restaurant falsely accuses Pigsy, as a punishment, it shall permit him to eat for free for three years.'

"Three years? Our business would collapse in just three days!" the owner exclaimed. Desperate, he called in a lawyer who charged ten thousand dollars an hour—a middle-aged woman of Asian descent. She smiled faintly, parted her red lips, and with a few well-chosen words, stunned the entire courtroom.

She said, "According to our investigation, Mr. Pigsy tried to steal the restaurant's prized possession—a high-tech, bio-engineered GMO peach—to smuggle it back to China via Monkey-King. Fortunately, patriotic restaurant staff intervened and stopped him. Had Pigsy succeeded in leaving, it would have been too late! Monkey-King, already prepared, was waiting outside for the handoff. With the peach in hand, a single somersault could have transported him back to the Chinese empire, and America's ten-year investment in intellectual property would have been lost!"

Our readers must realize that the absurd intellectual property issues are usually a headache for every judge. Whenever disputes reach this level, there is undoubtedly a long, arduous road ahead.

The judge, visibly shaken, paused briefly before solemnly banging his gavel again and said, "This case has grown more complicated. The court is adjourned for now. Why don't you all consider settling out of court?"

At this moment, the reader might be impressed by the woman lawyer's statement. No surprise, she is from another Ivy League school near NYC. Her statement has a sensational effect, which echoes the recent American media's false claim of Chinese theft of US technology. She was definitely worth the $10,000/hour fee in irony.

Monkey-King turned to Adam and remarked, "So this is what an elite American lawyer can do—turn black into white, distort facts, and stir up confusion."

Adam responded with pride, "In America, lawyers are like basketball players. Ordinary players can score from under the hoop, but elite ones can make half-court shots. Lawyers do not concern themselves with justice or morality—just as a player doesn't care where the ball comes from. Winning is all that matters, by any tricks necessary. But fear not! The judge acts as the referee, ensuring fairness based on rules."

Monkey-King frowned. "I am a disciple of the Buddha, and I do things openly and honorably. I do not say things that are not true. How should I counter this?"

Adam smirked. He said, "Let me give you some advice. That restaurant owner, having lost his business, is now desperate and will stop at nothing to fight. Pigsy may be strong, but he lacks strategy—this is what the Chinese call in the situation, 'a hero with no place to use his strength.' I've heard that in China, people favor the saying 'Of the Thirty-Six Stratagems, running away is the best.' Given the current situation, Pigsy should simply run away, just disguise himself, and make a quick escape! But if he pleads guilty and agrees to compensation, I can persuade the judge to give him a lighter sentence. Grant clemency, you know?"

Adam planned it perfectly. If Monkey-King and Pigsy admitted guilt and surrendered, even with a lighter sentence, this legal defeat of legendary figures like Monkey-King and Pigsy would likely cause outrage in China and alarm the world. Adam would claim total victory and become an American hero, a proud champion from an Ivy League school.

The Finale, the Grand Re-Opening of Buffy

Hold on!" Monkey-King exclaimed. "Sun Tzu's 'Art of War' says, 'The supreme art of war is to subdue the enemy without fighting.' Why should I battle them in court? Since the owner is only concerned about his lost business, I will restore what was lost, and the problem will resolve itself.

Monkey-King waved his hands to everyone in the court, "Gentlemen and Ladies, everyone, come with me this way..."

With that, Monkey-King chanted an incantation, summoning clouds that carried everyone—including the kitchen staff—back to Buffet Restaurant. When they arrived, Monkey-King created a magical wind over the area, and the restaurant miraculously appeared completely restored, shining larger and more magnificent than before. The owner and staff gasped in astonishment but were overjoyed.

Then, with a flourish, Monkey-King danced in the big dining hall with his hands moving up and down, side to side, sending dozens of steel serving trays flying through the air around him, shining like silver—a beautiful acrobat's show. When he finally stopped, the trays descended onto the buffet tables, each now filled with steaming hot delicacies—chicken, duck, fish, meat, fruits—anything you can name, all fresh and fragrant.

Monkey-King declared, "These enchanted trays now possess divine energy from the universe. From this moment on, they will never run empty. Whenever food is taken low, they will refill themselves."

"Oh, my God," everyone yelled in disbelief.

The Buffet Town owner was thrilled when he heard this. "Such a miracle has fallen into my lap!" He became very happy. Watching the enchanted, infinitely replenishing serving trays, his eyes sparkled with excitement. He burst out laughing and then hugged Monkey-King tightly, exclaiming, "I was blind to Monkey-King, the divine, and offended Mr. Pigsy—please, Immortal Master, forgive me for bringing you to court! You are my everything. With your visit today, I will now be the top buffet restaurant in all of New York!"

Pigsy, still thinking about food, asked eagerly, "So does this mean I can eat here whenever I want?"

The owner, along with the entire restaurant staff, clapped their hands and cheered, "Come anytime. Nothing would please us more! Nothing would please us more!"

The crowd cheers. Newsmen who had not stopped taking pictures and videos since the start of the event were all laughing.

Monkey-King turned to Adam with a smile and asked, "Is this story aligned with your Ivy League school teaching strategy? Is this what you typically call 'out-of-court settlement'? It's no different from our old 'private negotiation'—something every Chinese person already knows how to do.

Adam gave an awkward laugh.

The Buffet Town owner wasted no time. He ordered the restaurant to be decorated with festive ornaments, lanterns, and banners. A grand feast was prepared to thank Monkey-King, Pigsy, and all the reporters, police, and companions present. News of the restaurant's miraculous revival quickly spread throughout New York, attracting the city's elite and dignitaries to the celebration. The festival atmosphere was filled with the sounds of drums, trumpets, and a live band playing "America the Beautiful."

Dear readers, in America, businesses love to find any excuse to renovate their storefronts and hold a grand reopening to attract more customers. How could the Buffet Restaurant owner possibly miss such an opportunity? Yes, there goes a grand rebirth and a grand reopening!

To find out what happens next, stay tuned for the next chapter!

Figure 5 Pigsy said, "These villains bound old Pig; the marks of the ropes remain. My lord may examine them closely."

Chapter Six: Monkey-King Sails the Hudson, State Officials' Trick in Albany

Now, New York City, with its towering skyscrapers that block out the sun, its diverse yet chaotic population, and its relentless traffic congestion, was hardly a place for long-term living. Monkey-King, born from the pristine landscapes of Flower-Fruit Mountain, nurtured by heaven and earth, could scarcely endure such pollution and turmoil.

A Boat Ride on the Hudson River

There must have been some events in Monkey-King's life. On one of those sunny days, he took Pigsy along for a boat ride. Pigsy was excited to go. He had not stepped out of New York since he arrived.

The boat was beautiful. It had a sail hoisted. With a breeze, they started off the journey upstream the Hudson River to Albany.

Along the way, they saw mountains rising in layers, mist curling around them, lush forests, and abundant vegetation covering everything. Eagles soared high in the sky, fish swam freely in the shallows—it was a breathtaking scene of nature's beauty as far as the eyes could see!

The boatman at the helm was an old man with a red face and horse-tail hair. Watching Monkey-King enjoy the scenery, occasionally diving into the water to chase a few big fish, he found it quite fascinating and grew more curious. He was also puzzled by Pigsy's exposed belly and strange manners. He asked, "You two don't seem like American locals. Are you recent immigrants, new to this land?"

Good thought, sir. We traveled from the Eastern Continent. We often hear about how technically advanced and remarkably beautiful America is, so we've come for a look," Monkey-King replied from the bow.

The boatman straightened his attire and said solemnly, "I am a disciple from Brown, another Ivy League school, you just called me George. I have been waiting here for quite some time. Word of your extraordinary abilities has spread throughout New York, and I have come to meet you personally."

Pigsy grumbled, "Brown? I bet it's just another Ivy League school. We already ran into two of your fellows. Why am I always bumping into you guys everywhere?"

Monkey-King laughed, "But I do find it interesting to see the challenges from you. Adam has become our friend these days, though I am still a bit paranoid about the woman lawyer from Yale. She almost got Pigsy into jail for what you would describe as 'For God's Sake'."

Besides," Monkey-King continued, "It has been an excellent opportunity for us to experience American life. The customs and traditions of the East and West are very different. I've learned a lot these past few days here. If you have any interesting stories, feel free to share them.

"Bring it on, let's see what you got this time." Pigsy shook his head.

George said proudly, "Our great United States is the foremost among nations, wealthy and powerful, renowned worldwide for democracy and freedom. Not only do visitors from your eastern land of China come frequently, but even those from Southern Atlantis Arabia and the Northern Arctic Circle, Russian souls, regularly send delegations to establish good relations, exchange goods, and buy our planes and warships." His words were filled with pride.

Now, dear readers, you might wonder—who is this Brown George, and why does he speak with such arrogance? The truth is, he comes from noble descent, from a family of officials spanning generations. He took this opportunity to challenge Monkey-King and Pigsy during their voyage on the Hudson—though Monkey-King remained unaware of his intentions.

George continued, "Having been in America for several days now, have you found anything you love? Our skyscrapers, cars, and Western-style homes embody the pinnacle of modern civilization—surely, they are to your liking! I know quite a few of your countrymen surrender to these marvels the moment they see them. Am I right?"

My only love is in these mountains, rivers, and forests," Monkey-King replied. "You, having lived here your whole life, might take them for granted, but their true value is beyond measure.

Pigsy, rubbing his belly, interjected, "What good are houses and cars if they don't fill the stomach or taste good? As for me, I love the buffet restaurants here! Back when we traveled west for scriptures, we sought communism, yet we survived on nothing but plain broth and simple meals. Never in my wildest dreams did I imagine a place where one could eat to their heart's content."

Seeing the conversation go nowhere, George changed the subject to material abundance. "I have also heard that the people of China deeply admire our democracy and freedom. Surely, America's political system must be something that pleases you?"

There is an old saying, 'Only after having enough to eat can one learn manners and etiquette.' Monkey-King replied, 'The people of the world admire America's wealth above all else; its political system comes second after that.'

We had very different views and saw things from opposite angles. It turns out that Americans don't truly understand your perspectives, and you don't fully grasp ours either. Separated by an ocean, mutual understanding is certainly challenging—it all hinges on how the media portrays them, yours and mine.

The Journey Continues: Debate over Politics in Albany

As the three continued their discussion, the wind filled their sails, carrying them swiftly upstream. Before they knew it, they had traveled hundreds of miles. Suddenly, a massive bridge appeared ahead, stretching across the sky like a grand rainbow, radiating an air of majesty. However, as they approached, they saw that the bridge was crowded with countless vehicles, crawling along like ants in a line, stretching for miles.

George, the old boatman, remarked, "From a distance, the bridge looks majestic, but up close, you can see its rust-streaked structure. After eighty years of wear, with millions of vehicles crossing it daily, it needs urgent repairs. And if construction begins, traffic will be completely paralyzed."

"Why not create a public registry listing all the parts that need road maintenance?" Monkey-King asked. "If citizens were warned, they could plan their routes accordingly. This sluggish approach. By the time you reach home, your food will have gone cold on the table!"

"Identifying weak points in such a massive bridge is no simple task," George explained. "Even with regular inspections, issues can be overlooked. Community groups have long urged the government to inspect and repair a dozen such bridges along the river. Still, the state budget is dry, and officials only deflect with empty promises. My trip up north today is to lobby for funds to repair this bridge."

Monkey-King laughed. "Repairing bridges and roads is a virtuous deed in Buddhist teaching. But you, a single ordinary citizen, may find it difficult to take on such a challenge. Challenging the government with your empty wallet is like an ant trying to shake a tree. Since this is a noble cause, I can lend you a hand."

"Do not underestimate me!" George retorted. "In a democracy, even minor issues raised by ordinary folks, when persistently championed, can become a powerful force. Drops of water gather to form a mighty river, overturning mountains and seas. I've learned some of your eastern philosophies, too. Politicians even have to court our votes, and ultimately, power resides with us, the People. Haven't you seen how environmental movements have toppled entire industries? How even the wealthiest businessmen have been ruined, all starting from a single housewife protesting pollution in her backyard? (Love Canal Disaster) Or how a few student draft resisters sparked the anti-Vietnam War movement, which eventually forced President Nixon into a vulnerable position? Today, I am the one lobbying officials, but in the future, it will be them begging for my mercy and seeking my favor!" George raised his fist and vowed.

Monkey-King replied, "I have little patience for 'future' and 'later.' You go ahead and rally public support. If that fails, I'll storm the statehouse myself and deal with the officials directly! Hope you won't need our backup."

George secretly mused, "I have always heard that China favors 'mass movements' and 'human wave tactics,' yet this monkey seems to prefer individual heroism. Could it be possible that my Brown education has biased my perspective? I will find out later."

The City of Albany, Capital of New York State

As they traveled several more miles, the river suddenly widened, revealing a city nestled between mountains and water. The buildings were arranged in neat rows, with a few tall skyscrapers rising above. The streets were organized, and pedestrians and vehicles moved with mutual courtesy—nothing like the chaotic, cutthroat struggle of New York City.

Now, dear readers, American cities can be roughly divided into two types. The first consists of huge metropolises, housing millions, filled with tall skyscrapers and busy businesses. In these cities, wealth flows like a river, but vice and corruption do too— where the strong survive and the weak fall, and where people fight for every penny of life. The second type includes small to mid-sized cities, home to just tens of thousands of residents. Here, you find only a few tall buildings, a modest number of businesses and banks, and a population that generally lives peacefully—going to work in the morning, coming home in the evening, coexisting smoothly with neighbors, and following rules with civility. To truly understand America, one must appreciate both kinds.

Docking the boat and stepping ashore, George announced, "This is Albany, the capital of New York State. You may follow me to the Capitol to see how I persuade the state officials—my Ivy League school skills are not mere empty boasts!"

Pigsy hesitated. "Government offices on my land have always been places to avoid. How can common folk just walk in and observe? I don't like to mess with them. I think I'll stay behind and take a nap on the boat. Monkey Brother, go on ahead, and if anything good comes of it, be sure to wake me up."

Watching Monkey-King and George leave, Pigsy muttered to himself, "Bah! The bridge isn't mine, so why should I care? Once it's fixed, I'll walk across it easily—saves me the trouble." Within an hour, he was snoring in the boat.

An Impasse of Solution in Albany

Meanwhile, Monkey-King and George entered the grand Capitol Dome. The hall was dazzling—golden walls gleamed under massive chandeliers, and the chamber was filled with people, ordinary folks, which surprised Monkey-King. At the front, a raised platform held a group of men in formal suits. A vigorous middle-aged official, full of energy, was addressing the assembly loudly.

"The economy is tough right now, but thanks to this administration's tireless efforts, we have achieved remarkable results! Let's cheer for it!" The guy waved to the audience and then continued.

"We have urged our tax offices to work diligently and tighten regulations. That alone allows us to collect an additional six million dollars in revenue. Furthermore, out of concern for the people, we have deployed more highway patrol officers, issuing 18,000 traffic fines and generating an additional $ 2 million. Today, we gather to discuss how best to spend this $8 million surplus. Let us hear your proposals!"

As the official finished speaking, representatives of various interest groups rushed forward, launching into passionate speeches, their voices rising and falling like waves. Each passionately presented their case, debating with conviction. Each, in their own way, proclaimed this message, "Today's world needs a hero—who else but me?" Everyone else is the garbage.

A computer industry representative, eager to unload surplus stock in a warehouse, spoke with tears in his eyes, his voice trembling with emotion, "Education is the foundation of our future! Countless children long for access to the digital world, yet they are deprived of digital knowledge and lack computer skills. Buy more computers for schools! Fulfill the wishes of children and parents! Save our children from poverty and ignorance!"

A big cheer came from the audience.

A manufacturing executive shouted, "Attention, everyone! The world is progressing with technology! Training our workforce is a duty we cannot ignore! Establish an adult vocational center, enhance our state's technological edge, and secure our competitiveness forever! This is urgent!" Of course, deep in his mind, he secretly hoped the government would fund worker training, sparing his company the expense.

A labor organization shouted, "Raising the minimum wage now! This is urgent and non-negotiable!"

The business owners' association responded, "Companies are struggling, teetering on the edge of bankruptcy! How can we afford higher wages? The market is saturated. Allocate funds for research and development instead!"

The healthcare and insurance lobbyists, a powerful force, refused to be left out. They shouted, "Public health is a humanitarian priority and a national necessity! Fund widespread vaccination programs and protect people from the suffering of disease!" Our naive readers should realize that if this fund is allocated, they will likely become extremely wealthy.

One after another, groups advocating for the environment, women's rights, education, unions, manufacturing, firearms, and tobacco took the stage to deliver passionate speeches. The hall descended into chaos—a battlefield of interests, a grand display of democratic debate.

Watching the scene unfold, Monkey-King chuckled, "This is democracy in action—everyone voicing their opinions, passionately debating. It appears to me that, in what they say, three parts are truth, and seven parts are performance."

George nodded. "Politics is an extension of market competition. The law ensures fairness, making it no different from a marketplace battle. I have heard that in China, decisions are made through 'one-voice rule'—first drafting a proposal, setting a framework, then gathering public feedback. While this method centralizes ideas and speeds up decision-making, it stifles discourse and limits independent thought. Not sure how effective that can be?"

Suddenly, a group of retired veterans in worn military uniforms stepped forward and shouted in unison:

"Enough talk! We fought in Vietnam, braved the deserts, marched through Somalia, and patrolled the Balkans. We now return home broken, missing limbs, abandoned by our families. Building veteran housing is not charity — it's justice! (Though in truth, they were lobbying to renovate existing housing.)"

At this moment, George could no longer hold back. Along with several citizens, he pushed his way to the front, unfurling a ten-meter-long banner that read:

"Alas! The bridge is about to collapse! The transportation lifeline is in jeopardy! Every minute, lives are at risk!"

The crowd erupted in applause. With a fiery speech, George rallied support and then signaled to his allies outside. Immediately, dozens of activists in outrageous costumes stormed in, handing out photos and materials outlining the bridge's critical condition, along with a rendering of the new bridge.

Inside the hall, journalists—long tired of the same old political disputes—suddenly found this unconventional demonstration captivating. Cameras flashed rapidly, broadcasting the scene live to viewers across New York State.

Seeing the media attention shift, the state official in charge quickly spoke up, "Hi, attention, every citizen, I have always planned to allocate funds for bridge repairs! However, last year, a million dollars mysteriously disappeared..."

His aide, alarmed by the slip, quickly signaled him to stop talking, shook his head, and covered his mouth.

The official coughed and quickly shifted the topic, "Ahem! This $8,000,000 surplus was hard-earned! I navigated countless hurdles to secure it! It must be used on a project that everyone recognizes. Who among us doesn't drive? Fixing roads and bridges clearly benefits everyone!" He waved to George and the cameramen to move to the front and center.

Pictures are quickly taken with the official standing in the middle of the front row.

But the different interest groups refused to back down. The debate continued, escalating to a deadlock.

Frustrated, the state official finally declared, "Since we cannot reach a consensus, all you can do is submit feasibility reports, budget analyses, and implementation plans for your proposals! I will review them and make my decision. It takes time to review, you all know?"

His aide whispered urgently, "Each report costs $20,000, the budget analysis $30,000, and the implementation plan another

$30,000. If every group submits one, won't this waste enormous public funds? Why not settle the matter with a vote?"

The official agreed. Yet when the votes were counted, the results were perfectly split, everyone had the same number, and "an unstoppable force hit an immovable object."

At this point, George was utterly exhausted. His voice, hoarse from shouting, faded into the noise, lost in the never-ending storm of debate.

Some of you might wonder, "How did an Ivy League Brown-educated elite fail to secure bridge funding today? Are they supposed to dominate politics?"

The truth lies in America's changing demographics. As waves of immigrants reshape the population and the civil rights movement challenges the old order, a new era of diverse voices has emerged. The traditional elite finds itself challenged, and governance becomes unstable, leaving many decisions unresolved.

Monkey-King, always eager to see the outcome, sat in the gallery, watching the deadlock with growing anxiety. Sometimes, he felt hopeful; other times, he despaired with George, who was genuinely doing a good thing. He scratched his head, frustrated — no solution seemed to appear in this American democracy.

Yet the state official, a seasoned manipulator, looked over the room with quiet confidence.

"It seems today's budgetary decisions are extraordinarily tough," he declared. "Luckily, I possess a treasured family heirloom— 'Universe Omni-Decision Wheel,' which can unravel any deadlock!" he said.

Universe Omni-Decision Wheel

At his signal, his aides wheeled in a massive, tall, wheel-shaped clock, over ten feet high, gleaming with a golden hue. At its center spun a gem-encrusted pointer, glowing an eerie blue. The wheel's surface displayed eight trigrams—Heaven, Earth, Thunder, Wind, Water, Fire, Mountain, and Lake—while its outer rim was lined with numbers.

All was quiet. With a dramatic flourish, the official announced:

"Democracy is about equal opportunity! Every interest group has been assigned a number that I gave you today. I shall now spin the Universe Omni-Decision Wheel, and wherever it stops shall determine today's ruling. Once decided, there will be no further dispute! God bless you!"

Monkey-King gasped.

That's no ordinary fortune wheel — it's a Daoist artifact! It reveals cosmic secrets and calculates the best possible outcome amid an endless array of variables. I once saw this very device in the Palace of Laozi. It was deep within Laozi's Library of Heaven! How did this clever official come to possess it?

Meanwhile, George, seeing the state official use such a wheel device, let out a long, sorrowful sigh.

Democracy has ended.

Monkey-King frowned and asked George, "Why? The 'Universe Omni-Decision Wheel' may be random, but at least it produces a result. How does this undermine democracy? Explain it to me!"

George shook his head. "You don't understand. When votes are evenly split, the usual practice is to negotiate behind closed doors—that's how real politics works. But this official, ever the schemer, secretly rigged the wheel, ensuring that every spin benefits his friends and allies. I may have the knowledge to fix the bridge, but I lack the means to secure funding due to this wheel. All my Ivy League school education is useless in the face of this deceit. What else can I do but sigh?"

Hearing this, Monkey-King's eyes flashed with anger.

"I cannot allow this corrupt official to have his way. Stay calm—I shall return shortly!" With that, Monkey-King darted out of the statehouse and, standing beneath the open sky, chanted an incantation. In an instant, the 28 celestial constellations and the 12 spirit deities[10] appeared before him. They greeted Monkey-King as they usually do and were excited to see him in North America.

Monkey-King commanded, "I seek to do a good deed today, but a cunning guy tricks me."

See over there, Monkey-King pointed to the clock-shaped wheel. When that 'Universe Omni-Decision Wheel' spins, each of you must subtly adjust its motion to ensure the pointer lands on 'Bridge Repair.' This must not fail!

The invisible celestial beings bowed in acknowledgment and quickly assumed their positions invisibly inside the wheel before waiting for the spin.

Moments later, music filled the chamber, and the golden wheel started to spin. The entire hall fell into silent anticipation. The

---

[10] In the ancient Chinese astronomy map, these constellations were assigned to celestial deities to manage.

state official, unaware of the heavenly interference, smirked in self-satisfaction, confident that his scheme would succeed once again.

At last, the wheel slowed, and as the crowd leaned in, the blue pointer stopped—right on 'Bridge Repair'!

Thunderous applause erupted. The decision was made, and in the eyes of the crowd, fate had spoken in the light of day. There was no jealousy, no protests—only acceptance. In this US congressional system, once a decision was finalized, interest groups could do nothing but prepare for the next battle in the upcoming oversight phase.

George, who had been drowning in despair moments earlier, suddenly found himself victorious. Although he had boasted confidently about securing funds, he actually had no viable plan once the Universe Omni Decision Wheel was activated. Still, fate had smiled upon him, and now the spotlight was on him once again.

Wasting no time, George summoned the press and delivered a passionate speech, his previous gloom washed away in a tide of triumph.

Here goes a Poem to describe the scene:

> George failed to lock the wheel of fate,
> But Monkey gives a lucky state.
> When votes conclude with no ideal,
> turn, turn, the golden wheel.

With his task finished, Monkey-King bid farewell to the celestial deities and got ready to approach George.

Yet before he could speak, a sudden whirlwind ripped through the sky. Black clouds gathered ominously, casting a shroud of darkness over the heavens.

Alarmed, Monkey-King hurried outside.

"Something isn't right..."

What is this mysterious storm? What new challenges await our hero? Find out in the next exciting chapter!

Figure 6 They boarded a small motor–sail craft they had secured, heading upstream north along the Hudson River.

Chapter 7: Pigsy Fights the Black Wind Monster, Monkey-King Calls Santa Claus

My reader, Pigsy, had been sleeping soundly in the ship's hold for hours when he suddenly woke up with a jolt. He felt the boat rocking violently, which made him dizzy and unable to stand. He quickly jumped ashore to investigate. There, he saw fierce winds blowing, dark clouds swirling, and the sky completely covered as birds fled in panic. The waters of the Hudson River surged turbulently, while in Albany, households hurried to shut their windows and doors out of fear. Before long, the black clouds dispersed, leaving everything as it was—except for a strange fragrance lingering in the air.

Pigsy muttered to himself, "Where did this strange wind come from, disturbing my good sleep?" Noticing that Monkey-King had not yet returned, he decided to walk into the city to look for him.

School Children and Police Encounter

This was an ordinary afternoon, just before 3 PM, when school was letting out. Children played and chased each other outside the school gates, while dozens of big yellow school buses shuttled students back home. The American yellow school bus is very distinctive on the street. Whenever a child's home is reached, the buses extend red stop signs on both sides, bringing all traffic from different directions on the road to a halt in an orderly manner.

Pigsy was about to ask for directions to Capitol Hill when a group of children nearly ran into him. He quickly dodged out of the way, but as soon as they noticed his strange appearance—with his long snout and big ears—they were excited, as if they had just seen a hero from their video games.

One child excitedly shouted, "Goldar? I have so many Goldar toys!" (Referring to the humanoid monster from *Power Rangers*.)

Another boy corrected him, saying, "No, he looks more like Squatt! He can roar and breathe fire."

Pigsy quickly protested, "My dear little ones, what's all this about Goldar and Squatt? I am your Grandpa Pigsy! That fire-breathing trick belongs to Monkey, but roaring—now that's something I can do!" Hearing this, the children got excited.

With that, the foolish Pigsy puffed out his chest, took a deep breath, and let out a thunderous roar into the sky. His voice shook the heavens, causing the ground to tremble and the city's buildings to sway as if they were about to collapse.

Now, dear readers, although Pigsy might seem clumsy, he was once the Marshal of the Heavenly Gate and was later honored with a divine title in Buddhism. Clearly, his breath and voice hold celestial power—something no ordinary mortal, animal, or plant can withstand. The children, who had initially seen him only as a plaything, suddenly realized that the power was real. Frightened, they screamed and ran away.

A schoolteacher, who had been observing Pigsy from a distance as he interacted with the children, had already found him suspicious. Upon hearing his sudden roar, she hurriedly ushered the frightened children inside and called the police for assistance.

Meanwhile, Pigsy, still searching for Monkey-King, was soon surrounded by several mounted police officers. One tall and fierce-looking officer reined in his horse and shouted, "Who are you, troublemaker? Disturbing children in broad daylight—state your name at once!"

Pigsy quickly replied, "I am Pigsy, and my official name is Wu Neng 悟能! I just arrived in this city. My brother was somewhere nearby, and I am searching for him. These little ones admired my face and played with me happily—how have I disturbed them?"

An office input the Chinese character 悟能 into a handheld device, and an English translation appeared. The officer sneered and said, "What? Your name means 'incapable' (悟能), you must be an unemployed drifter. The city of Albany isn't like New York, where you can just wander around. I ought to take you to the shelter— unless you leave this city area immediately on your own."

The foolish Pigsy argued, "I also go by the name Pigsy. I run an Oriental martial arts school in New York City, where I wield my rake and train my disciples—eighty-six of them in total! Each of them is a formidable warrior, unmatched in battle. If you arrest me, they won't take it lightly, and trouble may erupt."

Unexpectedly, upon hearing his name, the officer paled, quickly dismounted, and bowed deeply. "I heard the name of Master Pigsy. Are you the one who plays the rake and has dominance in New York's martial world? I am very surprised to meet you today. It is truly a Heaven's blessing!"

Seeing Pigsy's confusion, the school teacher quickly interjected, "Apologies for any offense to the Master. We are on high alert these days. You know what, Master, for some time now, precisely at 3 PM every day when school lets out, a black wind blows over. It leaves behind a sweet fragrance that bewilders children, making them sick and disrespectful toward parents and teachers, causing students to refuse to follow rules and be disdainful of traditional games. In toy stores and children's bedrooms, strange little figurines have appeared—some with sharp teeth and grotesque faces, others wielding sharp weapons with a violent and terrifying look. Yet the children adore them, refusing to part with them for even a moment. Gradually, they are losing their sense of reality, unable to distinguish between good and evil, beauty and ugliness.

Another officer chimed in, "We police got a report, but cannot do anything about it. This Black Wind Monster comes and goes without a trace—we cannot catch it. Just the other day, even the FBI agents stationed here failed to trap anything but a gust of wind. If Master Pigsy can subdue this demon, your fame will spread across America, and the children's parents will be forever grateful!"

Pigsy Captures the Black Wind Monster and Demands His Green Card

Hearing that the demon's tricks were just gusts of wind, and seeing the crowd cheer him on, Pigsy puffed up with pride and said, "So, you all seek my help? Catching demons and fighting monsters? You've come to the right person. That's exactly what I'm good at! I live for that! Have you not heard how many devils I've captured on my journey to the West? Even my Monkey-King Brother was just my helper. I caught so many he couldn't tie them up fast enough!"

However, realizing that the only reward being offered was praise and gratitude, Pigsy quickly changed his tune. "Sure, I can capture the demon. But don't people say that foreigners 'Special Talents' can earn green cards? If I capture the Black Wind Monster, shouldn't I qualify for 'First Priority,' under some 'National Interest' immigration stipulation?"

The police sergeant laughed wholeheartedly and quickly promised, "No problem at all, that is an easy soup."

The crowd eagerly nodded. "Of course, of course! An absolutely exceptional talent! Go ahead!"

Pigsy snorted and dropped the phrase, "Don't you try to tease me!" Then he stepped onto a cloud and soared into the mountains to find the Black Wind Monster. People watched him below in the city.

Pigsy Fight Black Wind Monster

Now, dear readers, the traditional culture of America has long been intertwined with that of Europe, fostering a strong tradition of moral education for children. It refines character, nurtures emotion through music, strengthens the body through sports, and cultivates beauty through painting and dance. Legends of noble heroes, Robin Hood's courage and kindness, Snow White's beauty and virtue, have inspired countless boys and girls. The honesty of Pinocchio, the devotion of the Little Mermaid, and all these tales stem from European fairy tales.

Later, with the rise of American cinema and technology, beloved characters like Donald Duck and Mickey Mouse became everyday household names, bringing humor and joy to everyone. But sadly, the times have changed. In today's world of children, merchants and businesses are driven by enormous profits. They are blinded by greed and have abandoned tradition, selling grotesque and strange figures under the guise of 'individuality' and 'creative expression.' Innocent children, unable to resist these temptations, have fallen deeply under their influence.

In the Adirondacks, the remote mountains of the northeastern U.S., where few dare to go, there is a strange toy factory. Its owner, the Black Wind King, works tirelessly day and night to forge monstrous figures—each one ugly, fierce, and cruel-looking. Every day at precisely 3 PM, he releases thick black smoke and powerful winds, which influence children's minds, affecting them more than anyone else. The children are drawn to his toys and can't escape. Even teenagers become addicted to them.

On this day, after unleashing his storm, the Black Wind Monster had just returned and barely settled into his workshop when a loud voice rang in his ears, "Hi, my wicked friend! Bewitching many children, yet hiding here in comfort? Take this strike from my rake!"

The Black Wind Monster looked up and saw a large, long-snouted man charging at him angrily. Quickly, he grabbed his fire-forging staff and jumped into battle.

The monster roared, "Who are you, and how did you find me?"

Pigsy roared, "You blind fool! I am the Rake Master of New York, and today, I'm capturing you to trade my green card!"

The two fought fiercely, exchanging seven or eight rounds. Realizing he was outmatched, the Black Wind Monster suddenly swung his robe, releasing billowing black smoke that blinded Pigsy's eyes. Dizzy and staggering, Pigsy tumbled to the ground.

Just then, a voice boomed from the clouds, "Brother, do not falter! I have summoned the old dragon of the Western Sea to help you!"

Suddenly, thunder roared, lightning flashed, and a fierce storm of wind and rain swept through, clearing out the black smoke completely. Taking the chance, Pigsy jolted awake, let out a powerful battle cry, and took down the Black Wind Monster. He quickly tied him up with ropes and, in a few swift moves, destroyed the furnace and smokestacks of the toy factory.

Celebration in the City and the Governor's Secret

Back in Albany, the city burst into celebration. Colorful banners fluttered, marching bands played, and citizens—young and old—flooded the streets to welcome Pigsy's triumphant return. The state officials decorated him with red sashes and showered him with praise.

"This is a joyous day indeed!" declared the governor. "Just moments ago, a decision was made on Capitol Hill to allocate funds for bridge repairs, a project well-received and beloved by the people. Now, with the great Eastern monk defeating the Black Wind Monster, our schools are flourishing, parents are happy, and our citizens will surely rally behind us. My re-election next year is virtually guaranteed!"

Suddenly, the Black Wind Monster, now shackled, cried out in protest.

My toy production was fully licensed by the state! I paid all required taxes—why am I being arrested? You have an investment in my shop, didn't you forget?

The governor rebuked him sharply, "Shut up! Stop spreading unfounded rumors. You blew sinister winds and corrupted children! You have lost sight of the principles of fair competition. How can I, for the sake of mere profit, dare anger the people and cause harm to the next generation?"

With that, he quickly ordered the police to take the monster away, forbidding him from speaking a word.

Monkey-King Have Fun with Pigsy

As the rally ended, Pigsy shouted louder than the crowd.

93

Now, don't leave yet! Don't forget! Everyone promised me a green card! And my Monkey Brother wants one too!

The state official then declared, "Capturing demons and subduing monsters is indeed a sign of exceptional talent. This qualifies as 'the First Priority' and aligns with the 'national interest' policy. Tomorrow, we will report this to the federal government and issue you a certificate, a green card, whatever you wish to have. Pigsy well deserves one. No need to worry. However, as for this monkey-faced fellow, did you just say his only skill is tying up demons after you catch them? I heard he was even doing that rather clumsily. A separate skill assessment will be required for him."

Hearing this, Monkey-King laughed and said to Pigsy, "Hi, my brother, it turns out that on our journey to the West, I was simply your assistant? And now you conveniently get a green card while I don't?"

Pigsy gave out a laugh and made a funny face.

Turning to the officials, Monkey-King added, "I don't particularly care for any 'green card.' However, I am naturally competitive in fighting and refuse to be a second behind my brother. Are there any more demons around? Let me catch a few more and show this state official what I can do."

At this moment, an elderly teacher stepped forward from the crowd and said, "There aren't many demons left. But in recent years, because of the Black Wind Monster's havoc, Santa Claus has been kept far away and has not made any visits. Now that those grotesque toys have been cleared out, the children have nothing left to play with. If only a great snowfall could blanket the land, Santa would know that peace has been restored and would ride his sleigh here, bringing beautiful gifts and warm blessings to children and adults alike."

Monkey-King Summons the Snow

Monkey-King grinned. With a single somersault, he soared into the clouds, recited a divine incantation, and summoned the gods of wind and snow.

Immediately, a chilling breeze swept through the land, and thick, downy snowflakes started to fall, covering everything with a dazzling white blanket. Before long, the world had become a sparkling winter wonderland.

A poem bears witness to this moment:

> *Snow blankets the lands as far as you can see,*
> *A world reborn in purest glee.*
> *Demons were chased away,*
> *Children are safe and finally free.*

The Return of Santa Claus

As the snow settled and the wind eased, the crowd looked up. It's a clear, chilly night, and the Northern lights ripple across the sky in bright colors.

In the distant, bright sky, Santa Claus appeared, carrying a large sack and getting his sleigh ready to leave. The golden bells on his sleigh rang clearly, and his nine magical reindeer sped through the sky. Joyful Christmas music floated through the air, filling the town with peace and warmth.

Soon, the churches' choirs raised their voices in heartfelt hymns. Families lit up their homes with festive lights, and children leaped with joy by the fireplaces and under the Christmas trees, shouting:

"Merry Christmas!"

What will happen next? Stay tuned for the next chapter!

Figure 7 Just as Pigsy was about to ask where Parliament Hill was, he was almost knocked over by a group of children and quickly stepped aside. When they looked up and saw his strange face—long nose and big floppy ears—they cheered.

Chapter 8: An Unexpected Job Interview and Contract Bidding

It so happened that the New York state government approved funding for a bridge construction project. Due to years of lobbying and tireless dedication, George was honored with the position of chief engineer, managing an eighty-million-silver-dollar budget.

News of the lucrative project spread quickly, drawing a flood of job seekers and eager subcontractors. With vast amounts of money on the line, everyone suddenly regards George with admiration and ambition.

Monkey-King's Job Interview

On one of those sunny days, after Pigsy had returned to New York City, George invited Monkey-King to the bridge construction headquarters. He said, "I am currently hiring various skilled workers and am in great need of talent. I want to offer you a position. Why not submit your résumé? If you do not have a written document already, simply recount the major accomplishments you have achieved over the years."

Monkey-King thought to himself, "People say that finding a job in America is tough, yet here an offer comes knocking on my door. If a position is this easy to obtain, why not take it for a few days? At the very least, when I go back to China, I'll have some stories to brag about, working in America for fun."

He then said aloud, "Eight hundred years ago, I wreaked havoc in Heaven and was appointed the 'Great Sage Equal to

Heaven' by the Jade Emperor himself. I was responsible for overseeing the celestial deities and star officers on duty. I was the one actually managing the star rotation in heavenly order."

George chuckled and replied, "I have heard of your legendary stories. However, though the title of 'Great Sage Equal to Heaven' is prestigious, it was merely an honorary role with no real responsibilities. It may have brought you fame, but I doubt such experience is relevant to bridge construction."

He then continued, "America is a land of practical work; there are no idle positions here. Besides, you may not know this, but I studied at RPI[11], an engineering school by the Hudson River, for many years, specializing in global bridge engineering. They call me 'Engineer George'. I am not just some smooth-talking lobbyist."

Monkey-King was momentarily stunned and thought, "An RPI-trained bridge engineer? Whoa, from the first engineering school in the US. He is really somebody I cannot ignore. Is this guy testing my abilities? I won't let him look down on me!" His quick reflexes and determination shone through as he prepared to prove himself.

He quickly responded, "There's an old saying, 'Mountains were not hiked in a day, and trains don't move by themselves.' On my journey to India, I trekked over mountains, crossed rivers, and battled demons—all through my own strength. My efforts were never in vain. I even became the 'Victorious Fighting Buddha,' a highly prestigious and powerful position."

George shook his head. "The title 'Victorious Fighting Buddha' is still an honorary designation. It does not involve any real

---

[11] Rensselaer Polytechnic Institute, founded in 1824, is the first engineering university in North America.

civil responsibilities, like governing a region or maintaining public safety. Moreover, the job description lacks clear definitions. You said you fight like hell, but how do you fight? What weapons do you use? What are the benefits? Without clarity, it remains an empty title."

Monkey-King retorted, "But I am Monkey-King for life! I rule over Flower Fruit Mountain and its five-hundred-mile radius. That is a real position, requiring lots of experience to manage thousands of Monkeys, well-known to all!"

George scoffed, "Establishing a gang and proclaiming yourself king without legal recognition? Even if your name is well-known, you only belong in the pages of folklore. Pardon my bluntness, I know in China, grand titles like 'President,' 'Manager,' 'Expert,' 'Great King,' and 'Heavenly Gifted' are found almost everywhere. It is so often that they've become meaningless."

Hearing this, Monkey-King was upset. He shouted, "I have great powers and can travel across the heavens and earth! Why is it that after these years, I still haven't secured a legitimate, recognized job?"

George smiled knowingly. "I did hear that you once served as the Protector of the celestial horses,' a role where you raised celestial steeds to be strong and swift. Why didn't you mention that?

Monkey-King looked embarrassed. "That was a minor position, looking after horses, a low-ranking manager. I was usually reluctant to talk about it."

George sat up straight and seriously declared, "Great Sage, you are mistaken! The 'Protector of the Horses' was a technical position—an actual profession. The strength of the heavenly horses depended entirely on the dedication of their caretaker, who carefully monitored their health, provided food and water, and worked tirelessly."

He continued, "Working with your own hands to earn a living is honorable. It is far more respectable than those so-called gods and immortals who sit idly and profit without effort!"

He continued, "I have observed that in China, people adore government positions while looking down on manual labor. They chase easy wealth but shy away from manual work. If this mindset continues, the nation's future could be at risk. Farming, forestry, weaving, and raising livestock—these are the foundations of human livelihood. Honest labor is nothing to be ashamed of!"

The American Work Ethic

Finishing his speech, George pulled a document from his desk and handed it to Monkey-King. It was a registry listing over a hundred job applicants. Among the names were prominent American royals, aristocrats, and high-ranking figures.

He continued, "In America, look, we honor those who earn their wealth through hard work. We value professionalism and do not believe that some jobs are inherently superior to others."

"Just as trees grow differently depending on their environment, people have various talents and need to find the roles that fit them best. Some may be more skilled, while others may be less so, but no job is inherently beneath anyone.

The key is to do your best and find joy in your work. That is what makes the world truly remarkable."

Monkey-King's Surprise and the Bidding Challenge

Just as Monkey-King was about to respond, a janitor entered the room, quickly emptied the wastebaskets, and casually chatted with George, casually calling him by his first name without hesitation. The janitor showed confidence and ease, giving no sign of intimidation, which impressed Monkey-King.

As the janitor left, George remarked, "I have heard that in China, officials prefer to be addressed by their titles rather than their names. Calling them by their straight name often provokes their wrath, as they see it as a sign of great disrespect."

Monkey-King replied, "An official is considered to be superior to ordinary people. The higher the rank, the greater the prestige; the lower the status, the less weight one's words carry. That is why people prefer titles—they distinguish high-ranking officials from ordinary folk. The vanity of my countrymen stems from cultural differences, so do not judge them too harshly."

"When people needed my help, they respectfully called me 'Great Sage Equal to Heaven.' But if I ever slacked off, they would immediately mock me as the 'Protector of the Horses.'"

Both men chuckled loudly.

George then said, "As for assigning you a task, allow me to consider it further before making a decision."

George led Monkey-King onto the bridge, where twenty other men wearing hard hats were already waiting. After some polite exchanges, George addressed the crowd:

"Many have recently applied to work with me, and most are skilled basic labor contractors. However, this bridge spans over a thousand meters—who can identify its weak spots where repairs are needed? No one has been able to tell me so far.

I have now decided to open this up for bidding. Whoever can provide me with the most accurate assessment will win the contract. So be extra diligent."

A company leader, a Caucasian man, voiced his frustration:

"Government projects in recent years have focused on supporting minority groups in the bidding process under the slogan of 'diversify'. Now that an Asian monkey-headed fellow has entered the competition, are we just here for show? This is truly frustrating!"

George quickly responded, "Do not worry. This bidding process will be entirely fair—only accurate findings of the bridge problems will determine the winner."

Then, leaning in, he whispered to the company leader, "That monkey may be good only at tending horses; he really knows nothing about engineering. He has no funding, no experience, and no workers. You, on the other hand, have experience and manpower. The contract is yours to win. I brought that monkey just to show the public that my bidding is fair and I am following the contract requirement of diversification. He appears to be listening, but he really doesn't understand much."

"I want him to witness the power of American science and technology so that he will humble himself and eventually work for me. That would surely benefit us all."

Monkey-King Challenges the Doubters

Hearing this, Monkey-King called out, "Hi, do not underestimate me. Go ahead and inspect the bridge first. Let's see what you have got. A monkey from China may outshine you all!"

The audience chuckled mockingly.

Monkey-King certainly looks pretty confident to our readers, and we will find out.

Now, dear readers, while America claims to offer equal opportunities, an immigrant's background still holds significant weight. You need to prove your abilities before they can trust you. America is a country built by immigrants who have obviously brought their cultures with them. What they excel at often relates to the work they did before arriving in the U.S.

In brief, we may get these general pictures of the immigrants.

White Americans, particularly WASPs[12], empowered by the Industrial Revolution, dominate politics, the economy, law, and technology. Their authority is unquestioned, and they control the major engineering firms. Government contracts, often worth billions, are primarily awarded to them.

Indigenous peoples, though lacking technological advancement, hold the land. They establish casinos, refuse to follow regulations, and often fiercely criticize the government. The historical genocide against their tribes leaves the government too ashamed to retaliate.

African Americans, often marginalized in society, have learned to organize and fight for their rights. When faced with

---

[12] White Anglo-Saxon Protestant

injustice, they take bold action. Their protests, riots, and fires shake the streets. The government, wary of conflict, tends to placate rather than confront them.

Asian Americans, being smaller in number and culturally inclined toward obedience, prioritize harmony over confrontation. Most operate small to medium-sized businesses, filling the gaps left by larger corporations. While they benefit from minority rights secured through Black activism—such as diversity quotas in government contracts—they rarely lead advocacy efforts. Instead, they quietly enjoy the advantages gained from others' struggles.

The Bridge Inspection Begins

A foreman from the white engineering company stepped onto the bridge, waved his hand, and a row of workers appeared from both ends of the bridge. Armed with hammers, they walked along the bridge, tapping steadily as they communicated via walkie-talkies.

After a brief moment, the foreman turned to George, Monkey-King, and the gathered crowd, announcing:

"After a thorough inspection, we found 543 loose screws, 21potholes on the bridge surface, and 21 deformed steel beams."

The audience clapped and cheered, accepting the accurate report without doubt.

Monkey-King, however, intervened, "That was only the bridge's lower part. Why didn't you check the upper sections of the bridge?"

"They are too high to reach. We will check them once construction begins. This has been the usual practice," the foreman said with confidence that he was winning the bid.

George nodded. "The best engineering firm, the best of all."

Upon hearing this, Monkey-King plucked a handful of hairs from the back of his head, chewed them up, and blew them into the air, murmuring some secret codes. Instantly, hundreds of miniature monkeys appeared, climbing swiftly across the bridge's upper framework. They playfully knocked on beams with tiny hammers, screeching excitedly.

After a moment, Monkey-King waved to the little monkeys, and the monkeys turned back to hair and returned onto his body. He declared:

"After further inspection, the upper sections of the bridge contain 97 deformed steel beams, with no loose screws."

The crowd gasped in amazement and cheered in admiration. It seemed like no one could beat Monkey-King.

But George held up a hand. "Not so fast, not so fast! Who among you can determine if any of the steel beams are actually fractured?" He still hoped that he could give the contract to his old friend, the brotherly foreman.

Monkey-King's Ingenious Music Technology

The white company leader stepped forward and said, "I have a precious metal fracture detector that uses Nondestructive Testing (Electronic NDT) technology to see through steel. Please halt traffic for two days so I can scan the bridge."

"How does this flaw detector work?" George asked, clearly curious.

"The device uses ultrasound technology. It must be placed close to the steel beams and slowly scanned in all directions—up, down, left, and right—ensuring no area is missed. It can see inside steel beams and detect any fractures," the white foreman explained.

"That is really a wonderful technology! Superior to all. Isn't it right?" George claimed proudly to Monkey-King.

But Monkey-King laughed and said, "Why go through so much trouble for such a simple problem? You hold up the traffic for days. I have already solved it. There are fractures at both ends of the bridge. They can be repaired immediately."

"How can you see the fractures without even inspecting?" The crowd was baffled.

Monkey-King grinned and explained, "I don't need to see, but I hear. This iron bridge is like the string of a musical instrument across the river. When vehicles pass over it, which we see all the time, they pluck the string, producing sound waves.

If the tones are steady, bright, and resonate harmoniously in the five musical notes, not as Do, Re, Mi, Fa in your Western music, but Gong, Shang, Jiao, Zhi, and Yu,[13]—then the structure is intact. However, if an unusual noise arises or frequency changes, a fracture must be present. I have been listening for a while and discerned the faults without the need for direct inspection!"

George was overjoyed and exclaimed, "The immortal truly possesses extraordinary skills! Using a metal flaw detector to look into steel is already impressive, but this monkey has come up with a completely new method—using his ears instead of his eyes!"

---

[13] The Chinese music notes, similar to Do, Ray, Mi, Sow, La.

His method saves time and effort, removes the need to stop traffic, and is unquestionably better!

A New Proposal

The company leader, noticing the contract slipping away, quickly protested, "Executing this project requires reviewing thousands of materials. Mr. Monkey-King is unfamiliar with our language and culture. How will he communicate with suppliers and navigate bureaucratic processes? Our company has specialized in bridge construction for two generations, with deep-rooted expertise and a flawless track record. I urge you, the chief engineer, to reconsider."

George nodded and said, "You make an excellent point. Monkey-King, I see that you are used to freedom of travel and might not be suited for being tied to a single large project.

I have a plan that benefits both sides.

"This contract only covers the repair of a single iron bridge, worth $8,000,000 in silver dollars. But across the state, over a hundred iron and highway bridges need maintenance, yet funding is scarce.

Now, with winter's snow and ice making construction difficult during this time of year in Albany, I plan to first build a horse racing track in the warm, scenic South. It will generate the funds needed for bridge repairs. I have already arranged for land purchases, material acquisitions, and the selection of fine horses. Since you have experience as the 'Protector of the Horses,' I appoint you as the State Racing Track Supervisor—overseeing construction, training, breeding, and competitions. Once we raise the necessary funds, the bridge repairs will be handled by professionals. What do you all think?

Monkey-King's Decision

Upon hearing this, Monkey-King thought to himself, "So that's why this guy took such an interest in my old experience as the 'Protector of the Horses'. He had planned all along to have me manage a horse farm! How could I argue my way out of this? Oh well, training and racing horses can be quite thrilling. At least I'll have some freedom!"

So, he simply shrugged and said, "I won't argue with you all. Let's do it! Show me the horse farm!"

Using the information from George, he flipped into a somersault and disappeared southward.

The gathered crowd, now relieved that they would retain the bridge contracts, turned to George and expressed their gratitude with joy—a salute to a friend.

To find out what happens next, stay tuned for the next chapter!

Figure 8 Just as Pigsy was about to ask where Parliament Hill was, he was almost knocked over by a group of children and quickly stepped aside. When they looked up and saw his strange face—long nose and big floppy ears—they cheered.

Chapter 9: Monkey-King's Land Acquisition & Jeson's Doping Scandal

Monkey-King had bravely defeated the WASP construction company and was sure to win the contract to build the bridge. However, the old WASP George, secretly supporting his friend's company, invented an excuse—that Monkey-King was unfamiliar with the local language and culture—and assigned him to build a racetrack to raise funds for the bridge. Still, the most unpredictable things in life are the outcomes you desire. By a twist of fate, George's ploy played right into the hands of Monkey-King, for Monkey-King, who enjoys life with horses, freedom, and excitement.

After all, raising funds for a bridge is a noble act of great virtue, something a Buddhist should gladly undertake. In Chinese culture, among all good deeds, 'Repairing roads and building bridges' is considered the most benevolent act! Moreover, back when Monkey-King served as the "Protector of the Horses" in the Heavenly Palace, he worked diligently in the celestial stables and possessed exceptional skills in horse care. He raised the imperial horses to be strong, lively, and energetic. Why not take the opportunity to showcase his talents in America?

Monkey-King Arrives in the South

Without further ado, Monkey-King performed a clean and swift somersault, flipping southbound to the new job to build the racetrack. His quick journey earned the admiration of the Americans!

However, things did not go smoothly. The very day he took office, Monkey-King was furious. He quickly discovered that the building site had no concrete plans to work with, the design was left in limbo, and the horses and materials were just illusions. In fact, there was no sign of workers anywhere. As Monkey-King patrolled the grounds, he found government employees idling about, either wasting time at their desks or engaged in lively discussions in the hallways. Many of them had their lunches in three hours. Some were debating whether the Buffalo Bills, a football team, would win another championship, while others were excitedly gossiping about a new shipment of nylon stockings at Macy's.

Monkey-King was furious. He assembled all the employees in one spot, looked at them sharply, and reproached them:

"You fools! The state government trusted you with building this racetrack, and yet you're just lounging around doing nothing? They say America is the model of efficiency. Are you all just messing with me, deliberately making things harder? Line up! Each of you will get three hits from my stick! You fools are trying to copy what that sucker George did to me? Looking down on me because I'm a foreigner? Today, I, the Great Sage, am setting things straight! Those who were lazy and wasted my time, get this strike as punishment!"

American Bureaucracy Defends Its Actions

"No, no, please, you must not!" cried a middle-aged employee, who appeared to be a manager among the crowd. Seeing Monkey-King's anger, he quickly explained, "We are all serving the state government, and this is how things are done every year. We didn't know your Supervisor would be arriving today. You are moving too fast. That whole 'efficiency model' you heard of only applies to private businesses, not us civil servants. Government bureaucracies all over the world operate slowly; it's their nature, and there's no exception."

"If you don't believe me, swap the officials of America and China overnight, let them work for three to five days, and I guarantee the people of either nation won't even notice the differences."

Another official quickly added, "Sir, I had just heard of your appointment and was about to send out the official notice, but before I could, you were already here! Albany is thousands of miles away—how did you arrive so quickly? You truly are the model of efficiency! We cannot match you, but we will improve gradually—no, excuse me, immediately."

Monkey-King scoffed, saying, "So, it's laziness out of habit, not a deliberate attempt to cause trouble for a foreigner like me? Fine, I'll spare you the beating for now. But from now on, you must work hard and follow my orders!"

Also, I ask you, "The racetrack site is the foundation of everything, yet nothing has been settled. Why is the delay? Tell me the truth quickly!"

Bureaucratic Land Speculation

One group of officials hurriedly presented stacks of documents, piling them several feet high on the table. One of them reported, "Over the past year, we have scouted America's tourist hotspots and identified eight sunny, ideal locations for the racetrack. The plans were submitted to the State Planning Commission long ago, but we have yet to receive a response."

Another group brought forth additional reports, stating, "After investigation, we found six locations, but business tycoons, the owners, have shown surprising reluctance toward us. They are complaining about paying too much in taxes and fees. We have already excluded them, citing reasons such as poor transportation and environmental concerns. The remaining two locations were submitted to the finance department for approval, but we have not heard anything from them."

Right now, more officials have come forward with additional documents, and one of them spoke with concern, "The real estate developers in this state always exploit government land acquisitions, inflating prices to extract money from the state treasury (GOVERNMENT MONEY). But this time, it's even worse—they're demanding absurd prices! We don't dare decide on our own, so we've been forced to delay the process."

Upon hearing this, Monkey-King yelled, "Silence! You think you can fool me with all your fancy words? If these real estate developers had no inside connections, how would they know where and when the government was acquiring land? And how could they be so sure about my budget details?"

With that, he kicked the piles of documents to the ground and declared, "So many useless reports—how could I read them all? Please don't bother, I will personally inspect a few of the selected sites. Call those real estate developers at once and tell them to prepare for my visit!"

Swift Justice at the Government Office

These local government workers, men and women, had spent years idling away in government offices, never encountering such a forceful and efficient official. They were so frightened they nearly wet themselves, exclaiming in terror, "Incredible! Unbelievable!" before scattering like startled rats.

Once outside, they gathered their wits and whispered among themselves, "George sure knows how to hire people. Where did he find this monkey-headed 'foreigner'? He just arrived and already sees through everything! We'd better be careful around him from now on."

By midday, Monkey-King led the officials to inspect the land. Everywhere he looked, he saw large signs planted on the properties marked for sale, each listing an extravagant price. Some read:

- o Prime Commercial Property—Open & Level
- o Excellent transportation options near national parks
- o Once-in-a-Lifetime Deal—Urgent Sale!

As Monkey-King approached them, a real estate tycoon greeted him with a broad smile and said, "I am an old acquaintance of the state officials, a frequent golfing companion. I trust you'll look after me?"

Before Monkey-King could reply, a Cadillac sped up and screeched to a stop. Another businessman jumped out and quickly said, "I donate to every state government election—not for favors, just for equal opportunities."

Monkey-King smirked, shaking his head. "So, this is what they call a democratically elected state government? What a corrupt mess."

One of Monkey-King's aides whispered in his ear, "These two are not just ordinary businessmen—they are the political backbone of the state government officials; they are the closest allies. We cannot afford to offend them. The same government circle approved your appointment as a supervisor. We don't openly discuss these closed-door stories. If the media catches any of it, we're all finished. I trust you won't mind me telling you this."

Hearing this, Monkey-King thought to himself, "I came here with good intentions, a Buddhist mission of merit-making, yet I've landed in the den of worldly corruption. How can I keep a good reputation? Ok, no matter, I'll teach these businessmen a lesson. I will teach them a lesson. I will plant fear in them so they won't dare act so brazenly in the future."

The Land Gods Take Unusual Orders from Monkey-King

Meanwhile, the local land gods and mountain spirits[14] hearing the news that Monkey-King assumed the position of racetrack supervisor, and coming, had already gathered, awaiting Monkey-King's arrival. They had long despised these real estate speculators, who had grown filthy rich by gouging and inflating land prices. But to the businessmen standing there, they cannot read Monkey-King's mind. They think Monkey-King is just another ordinary government official, and that the divine beings are merely here to escort their Supervisor.

Monkey-King secretly instructed the land gods:

"I want to punish these real estate tycoons. You must help me. Stay alert. If any mistakes happen, I'll punish you along with them!"

The land gods, who had long harbored resentment toward these profiteers, immediately bowed and eagerly agreed, "Great Sage, you have come all the way to America to fight corruption. How could we not obey?"

Monkey-King then ordered, "Go investigate the land records and uncover every hidden defect on these properties. Add those flaws to the signs they posted over there!"

---

[14] In Chinese legends, these lower-ranking deities are all afraid of Monkey-King's temperament.

Without hesitation, the land gods rushed off to carry out his orders.

As Monkey-King and his team continued surveying the land, a sudden ringing sound echoed from the property signs. New lines of text appeared beneath the original advertisements, revealing major hidden flaws:

- Underground Cavities—Unstable Foundations
- Massive Rock Formations—Challenging for Pipeline Installation
- "Saline-Alkali Soil—Nothing Grows Here"
- Low-Lying Swamp—Breeding Ground for Mosquitoes

Monkey-King declared, "Transparency is the key to fair business. I have identified every hidden issue with these lands. Now, everyone can decide for themselves what to do next. Refresh your prices accordingly. But let it be known—those who once tried to cheat me will not get away with it again!"

The real estate moguls were horrified. They wondered how this monkey-headed official had uncovered such precise details that they themselves had tried hard to hide.

Now that the true state of our land is revealed, how can we sell at inflated prices? Who else will want them?

The two businessmen closest to the state officials had already done their research and realized that today's Supervisor was no ordinary figure. He had the power to shake the very foundations of the land deal operation. They quickly bowed deeply and pleaded, "We willingly donate these 'unusable' lands to the government—on one condition: that we get tax breaks in return."

The Art of Tax Deductions

To readers unfamiliar with US tax practice, you need to know that this donation may seem like an act of generosity. Still, in reality, tax deductions are a lucrative business strategy. When used wisely, the profits can be substantial. It is common for a businessman to donate $10,000 and receive a $3,000 tax deduction. But for those with the right connections, a $10,000 donation might yield a $20,000 tax break, effectively *earning* them an extra $10,000 in profit.

Since they could no longer sell their land at high prices, the tycoons chose tax breaks instead—how much they could get would depend on their political maneuvering.

Monkey-King responded, "Deception and exploitation are not the way of the Buddha. I will acquire the land at a fair price. But remember, greed must not blind you in the future."

Soon, the land acquisition for the racetrack was finalized at a fair price.

With the land secured, everyone eagerly threw themselves into construction. Monkey-King, using his divine powers, employed the Art of Transposition—magically transporting structures from the Four Great Continents of the world to the racetrack. He paid special attention to the Baroque Pavilion, dismantling and reassembling it repeatedly to align with the principles of Yin-Yang and Feng Shui.[15]

By the time construction was complete, the grandstand stood magnificently, leaving onlookers in awe. The race track itself was vast and level, ready for horses to gallop freely!

---

[15] These are the fundamentals of Chinese architectural principles. They balance 'Yin' and 'Yang' supposedly.

Monkey-King then set out to gather and train the finest horses, ensuring they were in peak condition for the races to come.

Figure 9 The racetrack was alive with extraordinary bustle.

The Grand Race Begins

Now comes race day. Old George arrived with his entire family, repeatedly praising Monkey-King for his outstanding work. "Have I not spoken the truth?" he asked with a chuckle. "Back in the day, the title of Great Sage Equal to Heaven may have sounded grand, but it was of little practical use. Now, after immigrating to America, your true talent in horse training has finally found its place."

Monkey-King was about to reply when suddenly, the sound of the race horn blared across the field. Dust filled the air as gallant steeds charged forward, met with thunderous cheers from the crowd.

Now, American horse racing is a primary gambling industry. The racetrack provides the facilities, but the horses are owned by their respective owners, who hire trainers and jockeys. Many of these riders had spent their days boasting and belittling each other. Now that they were face-to-face on the racetrack, their rivalry burned fiercely, each determined to win. Even the mighty thoroughbreds ran with unmatched passion after hearing about Monkey-King, the legendary Stable Supervisor from the Celestial Court of a mysterious Eastern land. All horses, all participants, old and young, wanted to show what they had. What is the most important of all? Each win means big money! Everyone is cheering for their chosen horse; everyone is betting on a big win.

Monkey-King watched, unable to hold back his excitement, waving his hands happily. Suddenly, one rider grabbed his attention—a man with a commanding presence, dressed in a black robe, riding a sleek black stallion that always led the race.

"Who is that?" Monkey-King asked.

A nearby attendant quickly responded, "You don't know him? That is the renowned Jensen, the Hero of America. His equestrian skills are unparalleled, and he has traveled all over the world, winning countless victories along the way."

Hearing this, Monkey-King's eyes lit up with excitement. "I have long wanted to meet the world's greatest warriors. Prepare my horse—I shall race against him!"

News of Monkey-King's challenge spread like wildfire, energizing the crowd. "An Eastern Sage versus the American Champion—this is a once-in-a-millennium spectacle!" Immediately, all the betting windows become crowded with quick betting tickets being thrown in.

At the betting counters, people swarmed like waves, pushing their way to place their bets. Gold, silver, and banknotes flooded the booths, creating a roaring wave of wealth. Across America, televisions interrupted their usual programming—sports games, rock concerts, soap operas—everything was paused to broadcast the epic race-track showdown live.

No one can resist the temptation; people everywhere stopped working and discussed this: "An Eastern Sage versus the American Race Champion."

The game was starting.

As the starting gun fired, ten magnificent steeds burst out of the gates. Monkey-King surged ahead on a pure white mount, its hooves like the wind. The stadium erupted in cheers.

But Jensen was no ordinary opponent. Refusing to give up, he pushed his jet-black horse forward, matching Monkey-King stride for stride. The two raced side by side, black-and-white streaks tearing across the track, blurring the eyes. Behind them, eight more racers followed, kicking up a storm of dust.

As they rounded a bend and entered the final stretch, Jensen's horse, Black Whirlwind, increased its speed. The crowd of 100,000 leaped to their feet, chanting "U-S-A! U-S-A!" The stallion's running form appeared unusual—its front hooves hit the ground together, and its back hooves moved in parallel, as if it were flying rather than galloping. In a final surge, it lunged ahead, crossing the finish line a full three feet before Monkey-King!

Thunderous applause erupted. Jensen, basking in victory, puffed out his chest, draped himself in the championship flag, and rode a triumphant lap, waving to the ecstatic crowd.

Victory and Death of the Dragon Prince Horse

Old George stroked his beard and laughed heartily. "America has long been the leader among nations, victorious in every battle. Who truly believes my US champion Jensen would lose to an Oriental monkey? My Ivy scholars have recently faced some defeats here and there, but at least we claim victory on the racetrack!"

With that, he descended from the grandstand to personally congratulate Jensen, handing him gold medals and silver trophies.

Monkey-King, however, was stunned. "As the former Celestial Stablemaster, I have mastered the art of horse training. How could I lose to an American I've never heard of? Who is this so-called hero, and where did he acquire such extraordinary speed?"

George saw Monkey-King's confused expression and reassured him, "Do not be ashamed, nor angered. As your own sages have said, 'Beyond every mountain lies another peak.' America is a great nation. Though you lost, you did so with honor. As we say, 'Defeat can still be glorious.'"

Monkey-King was about to reply when a commotion broke out—the horse, Black Whirlwind, which Jenson rode, had collapsed on the track, convulsing violently. The crowd moved quickly forward in alarm. The horse foamed at the mouth, gasped for air, and then, to everyone's shock, spoke in human language to Monkey-King, "*Your Great Sage, I am the second son, the prince of the Dragon King of the Western Seas. I broke heavenly laws and was reincarnated as a horse. Jensen forced me into races. Obsessed with wealth, he made me take heroin and elixirs and had steroid injections before every big race, pushing me past my limits. Great Sage, I meant no disrespect in today's race—my actions weren't my own. But now, my life is ending. Please, I beg you, tell my father what happened to me.*"

With those words, the dragon prince let out a sorrowful cry of blood—and died.

The stadium fell silent in shock. Jensen, still unaware of his disgrace, tried to defend himself, but the audience refused to listen. His medals and ribbons were taken away, and he was pushed off the stage in shame.

Monkey-King knelt by the fallen horse and placed a hand on its lifeless mane. He sighed deeply. "I have heard whispers of doping scandals in sports, but I never imagined even animals would suffer this fate. A man may willingly sacrifice himself for wealth, but must a horse perish for the same reason? True sportsmanship is about the love of life, not money. It is not a contest of who can create the most potent drugs."

George, too, was shaken. "You are absolutely right. Athletics should be about physical excellence and personal growth. But now, money has corrupted it. The winner takes home millions, while the loser leaves with nothing. Athletes, desperate for success, gamble their health on performance-enhancing drugs. This is no longer a local issue—it is a global crisis. Jensen's disgrace should serve as a warning to us all."

A Broader Reflection on Sports

After a moment of thought, George added, "But still, I would not rule out China lacking sportsmanship. I have heard that China, too, has its own sporting troubles. Your system focuses on training only a handful of elite athletes, while the general public remains mere spectators. These chosen few endure extreme training from a young age, pushing past pain and injury to earn fleeting glory. Once retired, they scramble to build a new life, becoming mere onlookers of themselves.

America's challenge is too much for the money; China's is a lack of individuality. True sports civilization is hard to achieve in either case.

Monkey-King opened his mouth to respond, but before he could speak, the crowd suddenly scattered in a panic. He turned back and was amazed to see Pigsy tumbling down the grandstand, knocking people aside as he fell through.

The clumsy Pigsy wailed, "Damned Bi Ma Wen![16] How could you lose to that fraud? You've made me lose every last coin I bet! I trusted you with an easy win!"

To find out how Pigsy ended up at the racetrack, stay tuned for the next chapter!

---

[16] The official title of the supervisor of the celestial stable in Chinese pronunciation.

Figure 10 Monkey-King charged ahead; his white steed was like whirling wind with every stride. From the stands came a roar like crashing waves. The American hero would closely follow—he whipped his mount again and again, giving furious chase. Black and white horses blurred the eyesight as they thundered down the course.

Chapter 10: Pigsy Sends Money Home — Elderly Widow Victimized in Land Scam

A Poem Says:

> East, west, north, and south—one globe we share,
> Mountains, oceans, and seasons, yet we breathe in the
>   same air.
> Believe it or not, distant lands all boast perfect skies;
> Each holds its flaws, its truths, its hidden whys.

A Hero Returns with Pride

Now, let's turn to Pigsy.

After subduing the Black Wind Demon in Albany, he bid farewell to Monkey-King and made his way back to his Eastern Martial Arts School in New York.

This time, however, he returned not empty-handed—but with a green card safely tucked in his pocket. Our readers should understand that the Federal Government officially granted Pigsy a green card as a Special Foreign Talent. Pigsy earned this by demonstrating his Gongfu. With his heart at ease and spirits high, he was a new Pigsy entirely, proudly glowing with pride wherever he went. Wow, imagine the tremendous applause the followers of this triumphant hero received.

Ivy League-educated Adam, along with students both young and old, took the opportunity to throw a grand banquet for Pigsy. They celebrated enthusiastically, announcing that Grandmaster Pigsy would now live permanently in America, and that his signature rake-style martial arts would thrive for generations.

The Power of a Green Card

Dear reader, never underestimate the power of a green card.

With one, a person can step forward into U.S. citizenship and access a wide range of benefits. Without it, even after living in America for years, you're still seen as an outsider. Without the card, you can still return to China, but you might be mocked as a failure and feel ashamed to face family and friends. They might see you as unable to survive and stay in the US.

Besides, in these turbulent times, conflict has spiraled out of control across nations. Refugees and illegal immigrants by the thousands and millions flock to America in search of safety. The United States of America, though celebrated as the land of the free, struggles under the burden of its extensive borders.

In recent years, the U.S. Congress, responding to the will of the people, has passed wave after wave of anti-immigration legislation. The green cards are made more difficult to obtain than ever, and have become a hard-to-acquire commodity. Countless immigrants strain their minds and exhaust their knowledge in their quest for a single card. The joys, the hardships, the sleepless nights—there are many stories about obtaining one card. But who truly understands these immigrants? Who cares enough to listen to them?

A Letter from Home

Shortly after Christmas and as Chinese New Year approached, the streets of Chinatown burst with activity—crowds strolling, lanterns shining, decorations popping up everywhere. Homes were prepared for the holiday; the atmosphere was full of happiness.

This is a fine day. Just as Pigsy was making plans for the festivities, he received a letter from back home—a handwritten note from Grand Gao, patriarch of Gao Village back home.

"To my son-in-law, Wuneng (Pigsy's formal registered name):

Since you left for the Western pilgrimage with Tang Monk, things at home have gone downhill. With no one to work the fields, we leased them to the neighbors and collected a small rent.

Recently, with this new 'economic reform' taking hold in the land, villagers have all but abandoned farming for business. They've headed to the cities to sell local products, including grains and soybeans, for profit. To make things worse, grain prices have fallen drastically for years, and now no one wants to farm at all."

Pigsy muttered, "What—want me to go back and plow fields? Life here is way better." He kept reading.

"Your wife Cuilan, while chatting with neighbors during her cotton spinning and clothes washing, often mentions how you were good at farm work and how you plowed the land and built mud walls. Those gossiping women around her exaggerated and added more stories about you.

"What started as harmless gossip was picked up by a writer from Guangzhou, who turned the hearsay into a book titled 'Pigsy and His Woman.'

"Cuilan was mortified. She cried and wailed, even threatening to take her own life. It took all our efforts to calm her down."

Pigsy fumed: "That wretched book-hawker! Trying to make money off *me*? If I ever cross paths with him, I'll rake nine holes through his hide! Poor Cuilan, she cares so much about her reputation, her skin is too thin to face this nonsense. She must've cried herself sick."

The letter then went on:

"However, in recent days, Cuilan has started to embrace modern ideas. She's been talking with the village girls about going south to Guangzhou. I don't think that's right. Our Gao family has been wealthy for generations—how could she go there to work as a laborer or a housemaid? But she says, 'The outside world is so exciting.'

"As a solution, I considered setting her up with a small shop—selling needles and thread—, but we're broke.

"Rumors are spreading that you've gone to America, made a fortune with your martial arts school, and are planning to divorce her. These words keep me awake at night and make me feel uneasy.

"So, my dear son-in-law, why not send some money home? It would help our household and silence those gossipers in the village as well."

Pigsy muttered, "So that's what all this fuss is about—money for the New Year. Well, good timing, I was thinking of sending the money to show respect to the old man and celebrate the new year!"

With that, he called for Adam, and the two headed to a New York City bank to wire the money.

The Tradition of Sending Money Home

Dear reader, Chinese migration overseas has a long history. Migration to America started after the Opium War—an era marked by a national crisis in China, internal strife, and hardship. Since then, numerous waves of migration have occurred, large and small. Some moved to the US because they couldn't survive in China; others sought their fortune through the gold rush; many are trying to gain skills and knowledge to apply back home. Gradually, this wave of migration has grown into a river—today, a flood of millions.

However far they are from home, busy with work, or burdened by hardship, overseas Chinese immigrants have kept one tradition—sending money back home during the Lunar New Year.

As the year's end neared, the scene outside the Citibank branch in Chinatown, USA, was lively and bustling.

Chinese men and women of all dialects crowded around the few banking counters, shoulder to shoulder, creating a sea of noise and commotion.

Banks and money exchanges, already aggressive in attracting customers year-round, would never let this golden opportunity slip by. Wads of cash flew across oceans in the blink of an eye—wired to every corner of China.

As soon as the twelfth lunar month arrived, staff were mobilized like troops to the front lines—counters packed, tele-sending machines humming in front of dozens of lines, though working day and night, staff and machines are still falling short of demand.

Outside, festival lights shimmered in the streets; inside, money changed hands in a rush of color. Cashiers hurried back and forth, hands full, ears ringing with bells, voices, and phones—all blending into a lively scene of celebration and chaos.

You might see a few Federal treasury officials helplessly watching billions of dollars flow offshore. They could only clutch their ledgers in despair. Confronted with a rising national debt, one such officer looked up to the heavens and cried, "Oh my God! Why do I have to go through ANOTHER Chinese New Year?!"

Roots and Reverence

At this moment, Adam turned to Pigsy and asked, "When I studied at an Ivy League school, I often heard that Chinese people send money home without even asking if it's needed. Generation after generation, this has become a tradition. Today, when I see it myself, it's no exaggeration. Their sincerity and emotion—why is it so?"

Pigsy replied, "For us Chinese, our parents are our roots. As long as we stay connected to them, we feel grounded. We have spiritual security. Our hearts are at ease. We fear nothing more than being disconnected from our roots. When your parents use the money you earn and send to them, when you burn incense for your ancestors, and when you're called a filial son or good grandson—that's your blessing."

"My monkey brother, Monkey-King, you know, he emerged from a rock—no parents at all. Every New Year, he grips his staff and cries. It's a heartbreaking sight, really, very sad." Pigsy continued.

Adam looked thoughtful and nodded.

All beings seek origin and return to their beginning. That forms a cycle of life. As you mentioned, it seems like Chinese people have a vertical connection with their parents— treating their ancestors as both a source and a resting place. Life and death, from generation to generation—that's a sense of continuity and immortality. It brings spiritual peace.

We in the West, by contrast, have a horizontal bond—equal and free. We all see God as both origin and destination. Parents and children each connect to God in their own way. Therefore, we don't worship ancestors, but we revere the Creator God.

Pigsy flapped his ears, "Nonsense, parents raise you with love. That is the debt you owe them. It is as heavy as mountains— how can you be that equal?"

Adam sighed.

As they spoke, they moved along the line until they reached the counter.

The Service Fee

A friendly bank clerk greeted them, "Welcome! We're happy to serve our valued customers. For your convenience, we now offer Express Lightning Service with a small fee to China. Only a 5% service charge!"

Pigsy frowned, "What kind of F--- business is this? Charging that much to send money over wires? I know the gods of thunder and lightning personally—they'd never ask for money to zap a message across. Are you just trying to scam me for your New Year's bonus?"

The clerk, momentarily caught off guard, kept her professional smile. She then said, "Well, sir, if you prefer to mail a check, that's free of charge. You already have a checking account with us. This can be easily arranged!"

Pigsy said, "OK, fair enough. Oh, I've run out of checks. You can give me another stack of free books."

"Additional checkbooks? The additional batch is $10 for a dozen," she replied. "Only newly opened accounts come with free checks."

Pigsy grinned, "No problem! Just close my account, give me my money, and I'll open a new one. Get free checks again – and save ten bucks!"

The clerk stood there, stunned and unsure of what to say.

Adam swiftly stepped in, "Master, why be so petty? Those free checks are meant to attract new customers. We've already benefited from that. Do we need to make an excuse to get it again, only to become a joke?"

"Master, if you insist, I'll pay the $10 myself for you — let's not let her think poorly of us." Adam went on.

The clerk waved her hand and said, "Never mind, it's on me. In the spirit of goodwill toward our Chinese clients, I'll waive the service fee."

Pigsy chuckled, "See, a small savings, sure, but a savings is a savings. A small sparrow is still a meatball. Now give me my new checks—I'll write one for $10,000 and send it off to Gao Village in

China. It's not that I'm stingy with my money... but if I weren't saving, how else could I have this money to give to my dear old father-in-law?"

The clerk and Adam shared a quiet smile, shaking their heads.

A Visit to the Elderly Home

After finishing their business at the bank, the two exited and headed toward an apartment building.

Adam said, "This is a residence for elderly folks who live alone. In America, people are used to taking full responsibility for their lives. When they can no longer care for themselves, they often sell their homes and move into apartments like this—to live out their final days in dignity."

"One day, you might find me here," he continued.

Pigsy laughed, "If you want to find ME, you'll have to come to Gao Village! The whole place is full of relatives, sure, it's chaotic, but at least it's lively and fun!"

As they talked, they suddenly noticed five or six elderly women crying outside the building, wiping tears from their eyes.

Pigsy was about to speak when someone tugged at his robe. An elderly woman exclaimed, "Master, help me!"

Pigsy frowned, "Who are you? Don't cry at the door—it brings me bad luck."

One of the elderly women stepped up and said, "We are all in our twilight years, with no one to depend on. Although we have children, they only think of themselves and visit only during holidays. Most of the year, we don't see or hear from them at all. Today, my son came by, and he just left... God knows when I'll see him again?"

"Wuuu..." she wept, and tears ran down her face.

Pigsy shook his head in disbelief, "How can this be? Where is your ungrateful son now? Let me teach him a lesson! After all you've done to raise him—how dare he not visit you?"

The woman indicated toward a man standing nearby.

Without a moment's hesitation, Pigsy stormed over, grabbed the man, and then SMACK—slapped him across the face, sending him flat on the ground. The man howled, covering his chin with both hands.

Piggy growled at him, "From now on, you will visit your mother every three days a week. Got it?!"

The man covered his face with both hands, trembling in terror, speechless, and nodding repeatedly.

The crowd gasped. The old woman, who had cursed her son moments ago for being heartless, now trembled and looked for a phone to call the police.

Adam swiftly intervened to stop her.

Cultural Clash: Justice vs. Morality

Adam addressed the crowd, saying, "Dismiss, dismiss! This master is a Buddhist monk from the East. His methods may be...

unconventional, but his heart is in the right place. Please try to understand him."

The woman, fearing she might be accused of inciting domestic violence, said nothing further and called someone to help her son withdraw inside the building. It was likely she would be arrested and appear in court if her son brought the case.

Adam turned to Pigsy and whispered, "Don't be too harsh. In America, children are not legally obligated to support or visit their parents. The fact that he comes on holiday to his mother is already considered pretty good."

Pigsy grumbled, "If this were China, the neighbors wouldn't stand for it! He'd be accused of filial misconduct and shamed into the ground."

He faced the crowd and said, "Grannies, don't be so sad. I just learned something today—You and your kids have *horizontal* relationships, not vertical. If you're looking for someone to rely on, you'd better go to church and worship. That's less trouble than crying out here!"

Adam's eyes became bewildered hearing this.

The Land Scam Revealed

At that moment, an elderly woman stepped forward and said, "Master, you seem like a kind soul. Please, let me explain, "We elderly folks live quietly here, lonely and forgotten. Not long ago, a stranger came to our door, looking friendly and familiar, chatting and making us feel cared for. Later, he said the government was planning to build a racetrack and that we had a golden chance to invest in this real estate project. We're isolated and uninformed — how could we see through his scam?

We invested all our life savings into it. Just as land prices started to rise and we wanted to sell, we suddenly heard that an 'Eastern Monkey-King' showed up to take control of the racetrack project. He forcefully claimed the land, paid us pennies, and took over. Monkey-King is now the heartless new boss of the racetrack.

Now that we've lost everything and can't pay our rent, the landlord is trying to evict us through the courts. That's why many of us are crying here, too. Master, you care for the old and weak—please, help us!"

Many elderly women and men begged Pigsy.

Upon hearing this, Pigsy's eyes widened, and he thought to himself, "So that's what happened. I never imagined the Monkey Brother showing up here and taking on his old role as 'Stablemaster of the Horses' again."

He then addressed the crowd, "That Monkey-King you mentioned, sounds like my brother. If it's really him, I'll make sure he gives everything back!"

Adam gently stepped in to warn the elders, "Scammers are always looking for lonely, vulnerable seniors like you. Lately, they've been prowling around old folks' homes, tricking people, and eyeing your savings. You must learn to endure loneliness and not believe every sweet word you hear. Losing money is one thing, but some are even worse, committing robbery and assault. Be careful! Besides, my rake-wielding master here has great magic powers. He'll help you get your money back for sure. But for now, just let us go and see what we can do for you."

The elderly women, hearing this, wiped their tears and felt greatly relieved.

Pigsy, though known to be stingy and fond of bargains, truly had a heart of gold when it came to right and wrong. With a huff of anger and a swirl of movement, he summoned a white cloud beneath his feet—whoosh!—and flew straight toward the racetrack in search of Monkey-King.

The crowd began to disperse.

A Poem goes:

> *In America, each child lives for self alone,*
> *While elders fade in silence, to the shadows they are thrown.*
> *Yet Pigsy, sending money to please his father-in-law's demand,*
> *Still finds the hours to aid old ladies with a kindly hand.*

What happens when Pigsy reaches the racetrack?
Will Monkey-King make things right? Find out in the next chapter!

Figure 11 As Spring Festival approached in Chinatown, the streets bustled with crowds; lanterns and decorations hung everywhere, every household was busy with New Year's preparation, and joy lit up each face.

Chapter 11: Spectator's Calm Withdrawal — Monkey-King Quells the Fire Despite Violations

Pigsy arrived at the racetrack just as Monkey-King was getting ready to race the heroic American warrior, Jenson. The place was packed entirely—people everywhere were shouting, placing bets, and filling the stands.

Hoping for a quick win, Pigsy caught the gambling fever hard, succumbing to herd mentality and a bandwagon effect; he couldn't resist his urge to bet. Besides, Pigsy knows that Monkey-King is superior in any horse race, given his history in the celestial stable with horses. Sure, Monkey-King will win. Why not make a safe bet? However, when he reached for his coin pouch, it was empty. So, in a moment of crazy logic, he pawned his heavenly weapon—the Nine-Toothed Rake—crafted by divine blacksmiths, to raise money. Our readers must remember that this heavenly Nine-Toothed Rake was made of purple-colored copper and had accompanied Pigsy in all his fights. How could he part with his dear weapon? All because of his belief that his Monkey Brother had always been the winner of all time!

The man accepting the collateral recognized Pigsy as the head of the Eastern Martial Arts School and trusted his name. He handed over 100,000 U.S. dollars (about 8000 taels of silver), letting Pigsy go all-in on the bet.

All Bets Are On

The racetrack was crowded with wealthy and influential people, and the crowd moved like waves in a stormy sea. Most American bettors favored Jenson, known for his military-style toughness and winning record.

Pigsy, grinning from ear to ear, thought, "My Monkey Bro has divine powers and used to work in the imperial stables—how could he possibly lose to these foreign thugs?" Without hesitation, he continued on his way. Of course, Monkey-King was invincible.

Just as Pigsy was dreaming of mountains of gold, the race horn blared, cheers erupted from the grandstand, and—run, run. Oh, my, it was a disaster! Jenson's black steed shot forward, leaving Monkey-King a foot behind.

In an instant, Pigsy's dreams went up in smoke. He lost everything—his money and his Nine-Toothed Rake. Furious, he yelled and stumbled down the stands, cursing loudly as he searched for Monkey-King.

The Doping Scandal

Monkey-King, seeing Pigsy's anger, quickly explained that Jenson had secretly used performance-enhancing elixirs to cheat. That helped calm Pigsy down a little. Nearby, old George and other spectators continued their furious denouncements of Jenson's ugly behavior.

Soon after, another horn went off—the next race started.

Pigsy, still bitter, muttered, "Losing money's not the worst of it—my rake got taken by that guy at the counter. I have to get it back!" He shoved his way through the crowd to find his rake.

A later poet would lament:

Wind shifts on the racetrack in an instant.

Fortune or failure, no one can predict.

One moment you believe the odds are in your favor,

See them leave in the next minute.

Fate destroys plans, like castles in sand.

Your wealth is set; don't expect any more.

Fire Breaks Out

A moment later, a sharp shriek echoed through the racetrack, "Fire! Fire!" Everyone looked up. Thick smoke was billowing out of the grandstand tower. Flames licked the windows and surged toward the roof. Fire alarms blared loudly. Wealthy spectators shouted for their children and hurried toward the exits. Horses neighed in terror, broke free from their reins, and galloped in every direction.

It turns out that Jenson, consumed by hatred after being exposed and humiliated, became a public disgrace. In a fit of malice, he set fire to the lower level of the grandstand as revenge.

Now, reader, if you think people panic during a fire alarm and picture chaos and trampling in the US, you need to think again.

In the United States, fire preparedness is a serious matter. Every building has clearly marked emergency exits. Schools, offices, hospitals, and factories regularly conduct evacuation drills, usually twice a year. Fire safety procedures are taught from childhood— *stop, drop, and roll,*[17]—and deeply ingrained in the public mind.

So, when the fire broke out, the crowd responded with surprising calm and discipline. People helped each other—young

---

[17] Pupils in the school are taught to stop, drop to the ground, and roll away during fire drills.

and old—quickly moving through all exits, which were clearly marked. Despite the 100,000 people at the horse racetrack, the evacuation was orderly, with only minor congestion and a few stumbles.

In no time, dozens of fire trucks roared onto the scene. Out of them leapt fearless firefighters dressed in flame-resistant suits. Ladders extended upward. Brave men and women positioned themselves atop the ladders with high-pressure hoses ready. In an instant, everyone took their positions. Water jets shot into the air. Mist and steam obscured the field. It was a full-scale battle between people and flames.

Here is a poetic witness

> A sudden blaze strikes the racetrack,
> Yet the crowd retreats as planned.
> Thanks to drills in the days of peace,
> No chaos erupts in the fire's blaze.
>
> With high-tech gear and jets of water,
> Firefighters leap into the fight.
> Flames twist skyward, ladders rise—
> A fierce battle between public safety and evil fire.

Jenson on the Run

Suddenly, the crowd erupted in a unified shout. Monkey-King turned toward the noise and saw a mob of people chasing Jenson, who was holding a lit torch and running in panic from one level to another, leaving burning trails behind him.

Monkey-King immediately lunged forward, shouting to stop him. Jenson, realizing his escape route was blocked by Monkey-King, raised the torch and launched into a wild attack.

Calmly, Monkey-King pulled a golden needle from his ear. With a shake, it transformed in the wind into a shining golden staff—the Golden Pole.

The two clashed. Flames danced, wind howled, and sparks flew from every blow. The torch and the pole lit up the air in a furious duel.

After five or six exchanges, Jenson realized he was no match. In desperation, he hurled the torch at Monkey-King and leapt away from the fight. Monkey-King twisted out of the way, barely avoiding a burn to his headband. When he looked again after the smoke cleared, Jenson was already gone—vanished without a trace.

Figure 12 Monkey-King plucked a golden needle from his ear, and with a shake, it transformed into the Golden-Banded Staff, which he swung directly at Jansen. The two clashed, igniting a fierce battle—sparks flashing, the golden staff stirring gales with every strike!

Unable to locate the arsonist, Monkey-King refocused on the expanding fire. However, by then, police had cordoned off the area, and all non-essential personnel were being pushed back beyond a 100-meter boundary.

Monkey-King, George, and the others were herded to the sidelines.

Frustrated, Monkey-King grabbed a policeman by the chest and snapped, "I'm the supervisor of this racetrack! I need to help organize the firefighting—how dare you block me?"

Startled, the officer pushed him back with his baton. "Firefighting is handled by trained professionals only," he said firmly. "This is an active emergency zone—not a place for unlicensed interference. If you keep obstructing official duties, monkey or not, you'll be in cuffs before you know it."

Monkey-King growled, "Isn't fire prevention everyone's responsibility? If you organized these people and harnessed their strength, it'd be a flood against the flames. Why do you turn our help away?"

"Utter nonsense," the officer snapped. "Firefighting demands specialized training. Do you have a license? No? Then stay out."[18]

---

[18] *To MonkeyKing, this was the language of no sense and surprises, because in China, everyone would jump into a firefight.*

Just then, two burly officers appeared from the fire zone, hauling Pigsy, who was soaked from head to toe and looked as if he'd been pulled out of a lake.

Turns out, Pigsy ran into the fire to try to help put it out and get his rake. But the firefighting crew, mistaking him for a looter, sprayed him with high-pressure water hoses and called the police.

Now dripping and shivering, Pigsy sputtered, "I went to save the place, and they doused me like a thief! Monkey bro, don't waste your breath arguing now. Let it burn—it's not our problem. Look around—everyone else is just watching from a safe distance. Just sit! The view's spectacular here, and it's not a smoke-free zone."

George Explains

Old George stepped in to clarify, "Brave souls, this isn't like in your land, where gear is lacking, and citizens are encouraged to fight fires with whatever's at hand. Here in America, firefighting technology is highly advanced. Even a blaze as intense as this can be brought under control. The public's role is to evacuate safely. Listen to me, if civilians get involved and get hurt, the legal burden is heavy."

That's why every building and public space has emergency plans in place. Trained crews respond to fires according to the plan. The rest follow the available protocol.

A Moment of Reflection

Monkey-King listened, a heavy thought settling in his heart.

He remembered the chaos in his homeland—how fire safety rules were often ignored, how people panicked during disasters, waiting for some untrained "leader" to tell them what to do.

"What use is a leader without training?" he muttered. "They only add to the chaos."

Observing the efficient operation around him, he sighed.

Here, contingency systems are embedded. When a crisis occurs, everyone knows their role. No need to wait. No need to shout.

This is wisdom. I need to take this back to China. I've learned something today.

Fire Out of Control

However, the blaze was fierce. The fire had broken free—spreading from the racetrack to the surrounding woods. Driven by strong winds, it leapt up the hillsides.

Fire fueled the wind. The wind fueled the fire.

Soon, the entire slope was engulfed in flames. Smoke rose into the sky. The heat was oppressive.

Planes circled overhead, pouring water in frantic passes, but the wildfire still blazed on. Their efforts were like pouring cups of water on a volcano.

George shook his head in sorrow.

"This fire... even with professionals, it'll take days to put out. That racetrack required so much effort to build—ruined in a moment by Jenson's flame." Said George.

Monkey-King clenched his fists. "Your system is good—but too rigid. Look at all the people here who *want* to help. They can help, can't they?"

He looked at the blaze. The fire was spreading faster.

He raised his voice and declared.

"This is no time for bureaucracy! We may lack formal training, but we have powerful tools. Let us try. See what I've got!"

With that, he reached into his robe and pulled out a brilliant palm-leaf fan, glowing with green rays and emitting a crisp, magical breeze.

The officer let out a chuckle.

"I've seen my fair share of firefighting gear. They're all based on combustion science—cut off oxygen, insulate heat, suppress flames. But this little palm fan of yours? You call that a fire extinguisher? Please do yourself a favor—stand back, unless you want to scorch your hair for an insurance claim."

Monkey-King's eyes narrowed.

"Ignorant idiot! Clearly, you haven't heard stories about me. I got this fan from the Iron Fan Princess while journeying to the West to extinguish the great Flaming Mountain, an eight-hundred-mile-wide fire you should know! The Iron Fan Princess begged me to return it, but I kept it for the summer heat. Never thought it'd be of any use here."

The officer's smile faded as Monkey-King moved forward. He blocked him again.

"Even if your gadget is 'new tech,' it still needs to be registered, approved, and certified before use. That is a Federal law. You think you're above it? I can't allow you into the danger zone with illegal gear!"

Monkey-King didn't reply. He pushed the officer aside, jumped into the air, and started chanting an incantation. In an instant, the fan stretched to seventeen feet, shining with celestial light.

Hovering in mid-air, he grabbed it with both hands and gave an intense wave.

Whoosh!

An icy wind blew down from the sky—immediately halving the fire.

Another wave— all flames disappeared like mist.

A third wave—a torrential downpour poured from the sky.

Verse to praise the magic Fan:

The palm-leaf sways, the cold wind sighs,

Infernos fade in silent skies.

Though equipment was plenty, none foresaw,

A celestial fan could awe them all.

The crowd below gasped and then erupted into thunderous applause. But Pigsy cheered even more loudly.

"Stop cheering, fools! If you flatter that monkey too much, he'll start flapping again—and next thing you know, you'll be airborne, flying all over the Atlantic with no one to reel you in!"

But his words only made the crowd more delighted. They cheered and laughed, marveling at this Eastern sage with godlike power.

Watching the fire go out, Pigsy waddled away to find his iron rake.

Monkey-King landed softly back on the ground, and immediately, firefighters gathered around him. They took turns inspecting the fan, passing it back and forth with awe. None had ever seen such a fragile and mysterious tool—each praised it enthusiastically.

Old George moved forward, eyes shining.

"Oh, you clever monkey—not only a master of horses but also a savior from fire! My admiration for you knows no bounds."

Watching the crowd pass the fan around in awe, he remarked as if he knew the fan very well.

"Clearly, this fan works by cutting thermal photons—maybe a breakthrough in high-tech insulation. Why not mass-produce them? Give it to every fireman!"

The crowd laughed.

Pigsy Got Injured

Just then, a stretcher team rushed past, carrying none other than Pigsy, groaning in pain.

What happened? Everyone was in shock.

As it turned out, when the crowd cleared, Pigsy was worried about his beloved rake, which was a deposit at the betting counter. Once the fire was out, he went back to get it.

Alas, disaster struck. A scorched beam from the collapsed building came crashing down and hit his arm. Now bruised and bruising, he moaned as medics rushed him to the hospital.

> Will Pigsy's arm be healed?
> Will he learn a lesson?
> What new wonders will Monkey-King
> encounter in the West?

Find out in the next chapter!

Figure 13 At once, they saw Monkey-King standing upon the clouds, both hands gripping a fan which he swung downwards with force. Incredible! A chill wind swept forth, and the towering flames of ten thousand feet were cut down by half. The people on the ground, beholding Monkey-King's divine power to subdue the fire, were amazed beyond measure and raised their voices together in praise.

Chapter 12: Tyler Boasts About Chiropractic and Monkey-King Challenges Western Medicine

Emergency Mayhem

Now let's focus on Pigsy, who was swiftly taken to the hospital by ambulance.

In the ER, chaos broke out the moment they arrived. A few women immediately set upon him, stripping him down to his bare skin.

Flustered, Pigsy grabbed his pants to hold onto his dignity and yelped,

> "Oh, merciful goddesses! Don't make fun of me—my wife would disapprove of this! I can't be bare like this."

The women, seeing this large oaf of a man so awkward and bashful, burst into laughter. They were thoroughly amused on an otherwise dull, busy workday. One of them tossed him a striped hospital gown, which he clumsily put on.

As Pigsy lay on the hospital bed waiting for a doctor, suddenly Monkey-King sneaked in from behind the door, also dressed in that same striped patient outfit.

Pigsy blinked in confusion.

> "Brother Monkey? What are *you* doing here?"

Monkey-King grinned.

> "I came to find you and return your lost iron rake. But hearing all the girls' laughter and merrymaking

in here, I figured I'd have some fun too. So I asked a
doctor for something to help my stomach. I haven't
gotten the pills yet, but they put me in this outfit instead.
Looks like it's the dress code here!"

The Checkup from Hell

As the two chatted, a nurse approached Pigsy with a
thermometer. She took his vitals—temperature, blood pressure,
pulse—then counted his teeth, checked his skin and hair. She also
holds a flashlight and shines a bright light back and forth into each
eye to examine the cataract.

Pigsy endured the fussing in silence, but just as he was about
to complain, the nurse grabbed his ear and started peering into it.

Pigsy howled,

Hold on—aren't you looking at the wrong part? I
hurt my arm, not my ear! Why are you yanking my ears
like that?!"

Before he could finish, another nurse shoved a wooden stick
into his mouth to check his throat. Pigsy grimaced and snarled so
fiercely that he looked like a demon. The two nurses got scared and
ran away, screaming down the hallway.

Dr. Tyler Arrives

Three middle-aged men in lab coats soon entered. The one in
the center looked like a senior physician and said, "I'm Dr. Smith
Tyler, head of emergency medicine. You'll need to be patient while I
take a closer look at that arm. And if you resist, we've got Narcotics,
knockout meds that'll have you snoozing in seconds."

Monkey-King laughed.

154

"My brother has a big mass and is as strong as a mountain—better use a lot of knockout juice!" He said.

Pigsy quickly cut in, "Don't listen to him, doc! Ever since I was a boy, I've looked up to doctors as if they were saints. Now that I'm here, I'll do whatever you tell me—inside and out, top to bottom. Just fix my arms quickly!"

Dr. Tyler examined the injury and stated, "Your arm has been bent by blunt force. We need to set the bone straight immediately."

Two assistants used two sturdy metal cables to secure Pigsy tightly to the bed. Then they rolled in a tray filled with shiny tools—saws, blades, drills, and steel rods.

Pigsy, still dazed, muttered but dared not resist.

Monkey-King, seeing all this shiny hardware, was confused.

"Back home, bone-setting only requires two wooden splints and a few weeks of rest. Why do you need all these blades and saws?" He spoke.

Dr. Tyler beams proudly, "Ah! This is the marvel of Western medicine. We use anatomical separation techniques. The human arm contains ninety-two bones — we disassemble each one, straighten them individually, then reassemble. If realignment fails, we bring in drills and rivet guns. All part of modern medical science. Far more advanced than your... rustic traditions. Now, could you step aside and let me start?"

A Surgical Puzzle

And with that, the three doctors began their work. They first anesthetized Pigsy, then disassembled his arm into several segments,

155

tagged each piece with labels—date, time, patient's name—and sent them to the Bone Repair Workshop for realignment.

Pigsy wailed,

"Thank heavens, I'm lucky it was my arm! If I'd hurt my butt, I'd be in real trouble!"

Everyone in the operating room started laughing.

Monkey-King couldn't stop laughing at his foolish brother's misfortune. He turned to Dr. Tyler,

"Since I've come to America, I've been having stomach troubles constantly. The local food and water don't sit well with me. It is probably due to *'water and soil incompatibility with my body'*. [19]Got any good remedies?"

Dr. Tyler responded thoughtfully,

"If you have stomach pain, we can remove your internal organs and hang them on the wall for inspection. Once we examine each one thoroughly, we'll find the source and eliminate it.

Regarding your so-called oriental philosophy of 'water and soil incompatibility', that stems from your Eastern belief in Yin, Yang, and the five elements— pure superstition. How could anyone take that seriously?

Monkey-King was speechless with shock, his eyes wide open.

---

[19] Chinese medicine emphasizes the impact of drinking water and the habitat environment on the human body.

Pigsy, in his turn, suddenly burst out laughing and goaded the doctor.

"Do it! Please do it! I wanna see what Monkey Brother's guts look like on the wall!"

Monkey-King waved his hands frantically.

"Cutting me open and exposing my insides? That'll upset my 'Qi' [20]and damage my essence—absolutely not! If you really want to help, have a look at my ears, nose, and eyes instead. My fiery golden eyes got scorched in Lao Tze's furnace—ever since, they tear up in the wind. And my ears ring, my nose is always stuffy."

Dr. Tyler replied,

"Tearing eyes, ringing ears, and nasal congestion all happen in the face, yes—but they're not connected. We handle them separately, one at a time."

Monkey-King shook his head.

"The body is an interconnected whole. You quack doctors only see parts, not the system. Treat a headache by focusing on the head, a sore foot by looking at the foot—how many people have you mistreated this way?"

Dr. Tyler replied,

---

[20] 'Qi' is considered the energy that enables life vitality in Chinese medical philosophy. It circulates in the body.

"If we try to handle everything at once, we risk confusion and distraction. Precision is important in Western medicine."

By now, Pigsy had been lying idle for a long time without any word about his arm. He groaned,

"Forget his wind-tearing eyes! I've been here for hours, and my arm's still missing! And now you're rambling about distractions?"

At that moment, Dr. Tyler stepped outside and quietly spoke with another man. When he returned, he told Pigsy,

"Eighteen of the segments have been realigned. The last one had to be shipped out to a bone alignment center for special processing, a thousand miles away. You'll need to rest here for three days while we wait for its return."

Monkey-King chuckled,

"Lying in bed all day? Just what my brother loves most! Don't rush his recovery—let him enjoy it. Just make sure you don't lose the package in the mail!"

Pigsy groaned loudly in exaggerated pain,

"Aiyo, aiyo..." he yelled, leaning on his half-functional side.

Monkey-King went on,

"As for my condition, these symptoms are tricky and unusual. I doubt even you can diagnose it. Let's save you the trouble. I don't mean to belittle your skills, but honestly, your kind of medicine? I couldn't care less."

Dr. Tyler's expression darkened.

"How dare you mock modern medicine, you monstrous monkey! I trained for nine years at Ivy Medical School, Brown University, and have run private clinics for 30 years. I master all the advanced medical equipment in the world—how can I let this nonsense stand a chance?

You're just a lowly Stable Supervisor from your Eastern legends. However, you have become a racetrack manager, still a glorified horse-keeper! Barely literate, it might be okay for you to hang around old George with Washington's dusty politics. Do you honestly think you can match me?"

Now, dear reader, you must understand—Monkey-King was born to be naturally proud and reckless. He strives for excellence in all things and insists on being hailed as "Great Sage Equal to Heaven." Back in the old days, his revolt against Heaven began with dissatisfaction over the low rank of 'Stable Supervisor.' He's always hated being reminded of it.

So when Tyler mentioned the title again, it hit Monkey-King's nerve.

Monkey-King said loudly,

"I may not carry a doctor's license, but I've studied the Huangdi Neijing (Yellow Emperor's Classic of Medicine). Our ancient wisdom isn't afraid of your clumsy machines!"

Challenge Goes Public

Their war of words became sharper and louder, quickly attracting a crowd of doctors and nurses from around the hospital.

Dr. Tyler, eyeing the swelling audience, saw an opportunity to boost his fame. Seeing that space was tight, he invited Monkey-King to the hospital's front steps, which face a large open courtyard.

Within moments, the building and courtyard became filled with onlookers. The entire hospital buzzed with excitement over an East-versus-West medical showdown. After hearing about this medicine showdown on the radio, hospitals in nearby New York City also sent their staff to watch. The ground quickly became overcrowded, spilling onto the streets.

Dr. Tyler stood proudly atop the front steps and announced to everyone:

"I, Dr. Tyler from the United States, am a highly respected physician trained at Ivy Brown Medicine and a master of Western medicine. Today, the renowned Eastern healer Monkey-King has come to challenge me.

Anyone who is feeling unwell can come forward. We will diagnose each of you and provide excellent treatment. Free of charge! Come to witness our advanced medical skills firsthand! And of course, find out who is the best—me, Dr. Tyler, or that Eastern Sage."

The crowd pushed forward.

Tyler quickly turned to a nurse and whispered,

"Choose typical but dramatic illnesses—let's make a strong impression on the crowd first."

Soon, the nurse brought forward a dozen men and women and pleaded:

"It's spring now, and thousands are suffering from allergies, mouth ulcers, red faces, swollen eyes, and severe constipation. These are among the worst cases. Let's see the experts at work."

Monkey-King observed the patients, their faces covered in sores, blood oozing from the nose and mouth—horrible to behold. He said with a stern voice,

"This is a case of internal heat. The changing seasons, with longer days and increasing warmth, have pushed external heat into the body, leading to internal fire and these symptoms."

The audience murmured in confusion—many didn't understand. A wave of "Ah, Wow?" rippled through the crowd.

Dr. Tyler responded,

"I've heard Chinese people often talk about 'internal heat' and 'internal bodily fire,' but I've never understood what it means. I want to learn more."

Monkey-King Explains "Internal Fire"

Monkey-King confidently raised his voice:

"The vast universe holds two opposing forces— Yin and Yang. All illness, at its core, stems from an imbalance.

When yang overcomes Yin, I would describe it as 'internal fire' caused by 'excess heat,' leading to mouth ulcers and reddened eyes and skin.

This 'fire' comes in two types—internal and external. Similarly, 'heat' has two forms—excessive and deficient.

These unfortunate souls today suffer from internal heat, with excess fire invading the heart. The excess heat is caused by the change of seasons. Their bodies have not responded well to the shift.

The crowd, puzzled by the depth of these rather philosophical terms, began to grow restless. Many shook their heads in confusion. "What's he talking about?" they asked. They shook their heads.

Dr. Tyler interjected:

"Scientific theory relies on measurable analysis. Yin and Yang are vague, ghostly, and inconsistent. If it can't be measured and observed, it might as well not exist.

"Science requires precise definitions. What exactly is 'fire'? Where is that 'heat' produced? A hundred explanations, all man-made doctrines and unscientific.

Regarding ulcers? It's simple to explain. Helicobacter pylori bacteria cause them. We use antibiotic cream. The infection will be cured. Data support this treatment. Case closed. Why bother with something as mysterious as the 'Fire'? No one can understand what you described as "internal" and "external"!

Two Approaches

Monkey-King shook his head:

"The imbalance of Yin and Yang enables bacteria to invade initially. Balance the forces inside, and the ulcers will heal on their own.

"I use niu huang jie du[21] Pills to detoxify and restore harmony—no more ulcers, no recurrence. Antibiotics treat the symptom, not the source. The symptoms return shortly after your so-called cure. Plus, bacteria develop resistance. Overuse renders antibiotics useless.

Tyler sneered:

"I heard a custom in China that lets small boys pee in the mud and play with clay to cool their Yang fire. Supposedly, it's a way to short-circuit body heat to the ground. Are you talking about the same logic?"

The crowd erupted into laughter.

Tyler sniffed and turned to the crowd:

"I won't argue with this Monkey Doctor. Here, each patient comes forward and takes my antibiotic ointment. Apply it morning and night to the affected area, and you'll be healed in no time."

---

[21] A popular herbal Chinese medicine to treat 'internal heat', reducing symptoms of sore throat, mouth ulcers, and gum swelling.

As patients started using the cream, their sores disappeared almost immediately. Skin became smooth. Pain lessened. The audience clapped and cheered, praising Tyler's amazing knowledge and skills.

Monkey-King watched grimly, muttering,

"These foreigners get fooled too easily... Selling shrimp at lobster prices!

Now feeling excited, Dr. Tyler dramatically pulled a shiny, inch-long scalpel from his satchel. It flashed in the light. He held it up for everyone to see.

"This blade has been my companion for thirty years. With it, I have sliced stomachs, removed spleens, reshaped livers and lungs, and even extracted bladders. Any organ—regardless of illness—is fixed with a single cut.

Would any suffering patient like to try?

The audience erupted in applause.

A poem to praise:

Slow Chinese doctors observe and feel your
pulse,
Fast Western doctors display steel gadgets for
cuts.
Both claim they're the best,
Yet, each holds the truth of one end, the other the
rest.

Just then, several more patients rushed forward, crying out in pain, "We've endured unbearable headaches for years! Each attack feels like we're dying! Please, either of you, renowned doctors, help us!"

Dr. Tyler narrowed his eyes—he recognized them.

He said, "This is a migraine. I already prescribed morphine and strong Tylenol. Take them twice daily, day and night, to relieve pain. Why are you here again?"

"Yes, Doctor, we've used it for years. It provides quick relief for a short time, but the pain always comes back and gets worse than before! Please, we beg for something better!" The patient complained.

Monkey-King laughed,

"Why, that's easy! I have **three methods** that'll make you feel brand new.

One: *Cooling Balm* for instant relief that lasts for 2 hours.
Two: *Silver Needle Meridian Therapy*—you'll be pain-free for a decade.
Three: *Axe Extraction of Wind Phlegm*—cured for life."

Tyler frowned in surprise and thought to himself, "I only have one method, and this monkey has three? He is impressive..."

He quickly added,

"Cooling balm—yes, for external use, harmless enough. As for silver needles, acupuncture works—yes, our Federal Medical Association has granted some certifications, though I still hesitate to recommend it. But 'Axe Extraction of Wind Phlegm'? I've never heard of such a procedure. No permits, no regulations. That one… let's hold off."

Hearing that cures might be available soon, the crowd was excited. Several headache sufferers hurried forward, begging Monkey-King for the cooling balm.

Monkey-King opened a small jar and applied the fragrant 'Qing Lang You'[22]—cooling balm—onto their temples. The scent drifted softly through the air, and their pain already started to ease.

Still, dozens more queued up to try the silver needles.

Monkey-King put on a white coat and rolled up his sleeves. He plucked a few hairs and turned them into shiny needles in his hand.

"The human body has invisible meridians connecting organs, limbs, and spirit—circulating blood and 'Qi', channeling heaven and earth's energy.

When these channels flow freely, one radiates with vitality. When blocked, pain and illness occur. There are 365 acupuncture points—matching the days of the year. With my needle, I remove the block, and pain disappears."

The Westerners didn't understand the theory, but when Monkey-King treated the patients, their migraine pain was relieved wholly and instantly. They danced and cheered for good reason— they were pain-free after years of suffering.

---

[22] A popular Chinese herbal ointment for headaches.

Suddenly, there was a commotion as a nurse stepped forward, leading several dozen women—healthy and radiant, with bright eyes and graceful figures.

The nurse announced on their behalf:

"In recent years, late marriage[23] has caused a growing issue—many women are struggling with infertility. It's become a pressing social concern. Among the crowd today, hundreds of hopeful women seek your medical miracles. They ask for your mercy— and your medicine that would enable them to have children."

Monkey-King's Witty Retort

Dr. Tyler was stunned—eyes wide, mouth agape, words caught in his throat. He stood frozen onstage. He will not be able to help with any of these.

Monkey-King laughed.

"What's the fuss? Why doesn't Dr. Tyler remove wombs from all these women and install new ones? Ha, problem solved!"

The women gasped in unison, stepping back with shrieks. The audience burst into chatter—buzzing, muttering, shaking heads. Infertility remains a no-solution issue to this day.

---

[23] In the Western world, years of education are associated with later marriages. The issue is particularly an issue for women.

Tyler said, "Wait, though this is hard for me, I can call my network for help. Western medicine has a network of professionals worldwide! We are not bound by family practice!"

Seizing the moment, Monkey-King said, "I have networking too. You want to see it?" With those words, he grabbed a large porcelain bowl, filled it with clean water, and blew a puff of immortal breath. He traced a mystical symbol on the water's surface, preparing for a dazzling display. He said a few magic words.

A Divine Intervention

Then came the moment— a clear, bell-like chime echoed from above, and blossoms began to fall like rain. Everyone craned their necks—floating down from the clouds was none other than Guanyin Bodhisattva, [24]seated gracefully upon a lotus throne. On either side stood two child attendants: LongNu and Shancai.

Guanyin spoke gently,

Monkey-King, your knowledge of medicine is limited—why show off here? It is proper to remain humble and keep learning. Chinese and Western medicine each have their strengths. They must complement, not replace each other. Especially in America, where health laws are strict and food and drug regulations are numerous, you must not act recklessly.

If your treatments harm the health of women or children, I won't be able to save you either."

---

[24] The popular goddess is known in China for fertility and bringing babies to women.

Monkey-King bowed deeply, discarding his water bowl at once.

"Yes, Bodhisattva. I accept your guidance."

Guanyin turned to Tyler:

"The creation of life should be left to nature. You must not overreach with your test-tube babies and cloned experiments. Seeking only short-term gain and ignoring future consequences, how can such a path be righteous? If you humans control all births and fates, then what purpose would I serve?"

Among the crowd, women recognized Guanyin, known in legend as a divine giver of children. Many hopeful women fell to their knees, praying fervently for children. More and more joined, chanting blessings.

Guanyin smiled and gently flicked her willow branch, spreading the magic water,

"You are all good and faithful souls. Go home and hang colorful baby paintings in your bedrooms. I shall visit each of you in time, and your wish will be granted."

With that, she slowly rose and drifted back toward the heavens. The people bowed again and again, giving thanks for her promises.

Tyler was bewildered and said to Monkey-King, "Oh my, I cannot believe your networking can go this far! I totally surrender to your magic power."

A poem was sung:

Auspicious clouds unveil Guanyin's light,
With a willow branch and a vase held in her hand.
Her heart of mercy ever shining bright,
She grants women's wishes throughout the land.

The Swimmers' Marks

As Guanyin left, murmurs started again. Suddenly, cheers burst out from the crowd as a group of strong young men made their way through. Muscles flexed, eyes shining—they were none other than the American National Aquatic Team!

One person moved forward and said, "We've been selected for the upcoming Global Swimming Championship. But my arm's been sore for days from all the exercise, and the doctors are useless. All they did was apply ice and give me some 'Advil' to dull the pain. People say Monkey-King has miraculous powers. Please, let Eastern medicine help me! We will then be at our best in the competition."

Tyler, seeing these star athletes, straightened up, eager to impress, "I never reject practical techniques from the East, provided verifiable data backs them up.

But arm pain? Eastern ointments often make false claims. Massage and bone-setting might help, but they can never fully cure it. That's a fact supported by data... Recently, I've heard of acupuncture and similar therapies. They seem promising, but clinical evidence is still lacking. And friends, please don't make things difficult for Dr. Monkey-King here. In this country, treating muscles and bones requires a license. This isn't like China, where anyone can sell secret family remedies on the street!"

Tyler thought to himself, "Getting that license would take at least five years. By then, Monkey-King will have flown back to the East for his good!"

But Monkey-King laughed heartily and said, "Ignorance! Eastern medicine has thrived for thousands of years, passed down with honor, father to son. In ancient farming days, this was survival! And today, China's medical system is just as regulated as yours. Doctors get licenses, and hospitals are modern. But let's not get bogged down in the licensing red tape. I'll use a simple trick—no need to pierce the skin or break bones. Come, young man! Try my ancient remedy: *Fire Cupping Therapy*! Passed down for millennia—harmless and effective!"

With that, Monkey-King snapped his fingers—and five glass cups materialized, along with a bundle of medicinal herb Aicao.[25]

He lit the Aicao, warmed each cup over the flame, and then gently placed them on the athlete's sore arm.

The crowd leaned forward, eyes wide with anticipation, holding their breath, waiting for a miracle.

Moments later, Monkey-King snapped off the cups with a satisfying "pop!" The athlete immediately stretched and rotated his arm with ease.

"What a relief!" the swimmer exclaimed. "The pain's completely gone!"

The audience erupted with excitement. Cheers echoed through the room. Others jumped onto the stage, pleading to be next.

[14.] The herbal-burning therapy in Chinese traditional medicine to treat muscle strain.

After the treatment, the swimmers strutted proudly, showing off the red circular marks left by the cups to their friends around the world. The crowd admired amid the noise of "Oohs" and "Aahs".

Tyler Takes Note

Dr. Tyler watched silently and nodded in awe.

"Where on earth did this monkey learn all of this? I've never heard of this 'fire cupping' therapy technique. Hmm... I suspect it works by creating a vacuum, heating the air inside, then letting it cool while sealed. Sounds scientifically plausible! This is a discovery! If I study this, gather data, and publish a paper, why, I'd shake up the academic world!" He thought.

What happens next? Will Monkey-King face more challenges in the West? Can Tyler learn Eastern methods? Find out in the next chapter!

Figure 14 Confronted with so many instruments, Monkey-King was greatly perplexed and asked, "Why, in setting bones, has it ever been using two wooden boards to clamp the arm, and in ten days or half a month it straightens—what need is there for all these steel blades and iron saws?"

Chapter 13: Pigsy's Wife Cooks While Monkey-King Explores the Post Office

A Wife's Arrival from Afar

Pigsy lay in bed, one arm missing, staring out the window under the moonlight, dreaming of his home, the old Gao village.

Dawn arrived, and with some noise, he opened his eyes—there stood Gao Cuilan, his wife, at his bedside, a basket of eggs still hanging from her arm.

What had happened? It turned out that Monkey-King, seeing his brother bedridden and uncared for, felt a pang of sympathy. "Brothers are as limbs," as the old Chinese saying goes. He wasted no time. He summoned Heaven's Four Heavenly Kings and ordered them to fly Pigsy's wife, Cuilan, from Gao Village to the American hospital, despite the need to cross mountains and oceans, riding the wind, all in a hurry.

Cuilan, now seeing her husband missing an arm and in bad shape, burst into tears immediately.

Pigsy said, "Don't cry now. It's just an arm. They've taken it to be fixed—no telling when it'll be back. If I'd known you were coming, you could've brought some healing paste; it'd work better than all this quack."

Cuilan suggested, "Once they reattach it, let's go home. I'll take good care of you in the village." The two gabbed away, talking about home, neighbors, and all the village gossip.

Taste of the Homeland

Meanwhile, Monkey-King thanked the Four Kings and opened Cuilan's bundled bag; his eyes lit up immediately.

Inside, he found a portable rice cooker, a gas burner, cabbage, peppers, radish tops, ginger, pickled vegetables, tofu custard, millet, sorghum, soy sauce, vinegar, and oil. Famished, Monkey-King popped some candied fruits into his mouth and munched contentedly.

"Aha! The flavor of China! So fresh, so authentic! The real taste!" Pigsy said joyfully.

That late morning, when the sunlight gets stronger, Dr. Tyler enters the room. He immediately freezes at the sight of a woman cooking over an improvised gas stove inside the hospital room.

"What's going on here?" he asked, confused.

Monkey-King recounted Cuilan's long journey to nurse her husband and noted that it is common in China for a wife to care for her sick husband in the hospital.

But Dr. Tyler was utterly shocked, saying, "I thought Chinese society was conservative in marital relations. How is this public display happening, and you're turning the hospital ward into a habitation?!"

Monkey-King burst into laughter. Cuilan blushed and quickly looked away.

Pigsy said, "I haven't had a decent meal in two days! They've filled me with ice water and random pills; it's a wonder I'm still alive and kicking. Thank the heavens for my woman here now!"

Monkey-King said, "My brother feels better today because someone who loves him is here and taking care of him. In China, the family stays by the patient's side. We eat together, sleep nearby. It's a way of caring. Even the neighbors come to check frequently to see if there is anything they can help with."

Tyler, with his arms crossed, replied solemnly:

> "That might work in your country, but here in America, patient care is a science. Only trained professionals may assist.

> "Our hospitals are completely closed systems. Patient vital signs are monitored continuously throughout the day. Every bite of food is recorded. Every nap and its snooze are tracked and documented. Every bowel movement is charted. Interference from outsiders with the system is forbidden. You guys are crazy for cooking on gas burners in hallways?! Absolutely insane! You are disrupting my medical system!"

Pigsy huffed:

> "What system? This feels like a prison! Give me back my arm, I'm going home!"

Monkey-King responded:

> "Your system is efficient, but it lacks heart. Emotional well-being is important. When a patient sees family, hears their voice, or feels their presence, that's healing too!"

Tyler paused, lost in thought.

Why? Truth be told, American medical circles are currently debating whether emotional support influences recovery rates — and Tyler himself is leading a research team gathering such data these days.

The Helicopter Surprise and The Postal Predicament

Just then—WHOOM! —A loud thump shook the building. Everyone rushed to the window. A helicopter hovered, lowering a parcel via parachute.

Hospital staff retrieved it. On the box, it reads, "PIGSY – ARM BONE #19, in care of Dr. Tyler."

Dr. Tyler's eyes lit up. He tore open the box and found a packing list—only to go pale. Inside were several silver ingots, a set of false teeth, but no arm bone in sight.

A note was tucked inside:

Dear Mr. Pigsy,
    Your parcel was damaged during transit. Sorry to
    hear your arm bone is lost.
    Please accept eight taels of silver as compensation
    from the mail delivery service. Complimentary false
    teeth included. Sincere apologies, best wishes, and
    good luck!

My dear readers, the United States postal system is robust. Mail services operated in both the public and private sectors, with overnight express services flying at lightning speed and ground mail crawling for weeks on end.

Whether in the city or the countryside, mail arrives daily at every doorstep. Still, with millions of tons of parcels zipping across thousands of miles, delays and losses are inevitable.

This time, Pigsy's original arm bone went missing.

Pigsy raged:

"If I go back to China, missing an arm, how will I face my neighbors? They'll think I lost a duel or got beaten up! I've fought a hundred demons, defeated dozens of heroes, and never once came up short of body parts. Now I return home looking like a loser?!"

Dr. Tyler, looking quite guilty, said:

"I understand you, Pigsy. Chinese people, no matter where life takes them abroad, always want to return home in glory. I'll organize a thorough search for your lost arm, with all hands on deck, and leave no stone unturned. And if the worst happens, my insurance for my medical practice will provide generous compensation—you'll still come back wealthy and well-off."

Pigsy shouted, "Who cares about silver dollars?! I want my bones back! Maybe someone stole them just to embarrass me!"

A Clever Suggestion

Cuilan, listening quietly, finally spoke up to Monkey-King:

"These foreign strangers mean well, but they're not our kin. They'll never search with full heart and soul. Brother, only your divine powers can help now. Please help my husband, your brother, be whole again."

Monkey-King (grinning) teased, "Aha! Look at how clever you've become. Sending me away so you and your man can get cozy, huh? Fine, I'll go with Tyler to work on this myself."

Tyler looked at Cuilan and offered:

"You can cook at the Eastern Martial Arts Studio and then deliver meals to the hospital. I'll arrange a cab for you. This is a special exception—not everyone gets this privilege. My apologies for the missing arm bones of your husband."

He also told the nurse to record Cuilan's activities—such as the number of visits, the duration of her stays, and her actions—all as part of his research on emotional recovery.

With roles assigned to each member, the party split up to take action.

At the Post Office Headquarters

Monkey-King and Tyler arrived at the Central Post Office, a granite building with "UNITED STATES POST OFFICE" chiseled across the top beam on the facade.

Blue metal mailboxes lined the front street, each bearing the emblem of a bald eagle flying, fierce-eyed, wings half-spread. Delivery vans move in and out—a constant bustle.

Tyler, visibly relieved, regained energy and said to Monkey-King:

"This is the pride of the nation. In the United States, every business is private, including airlines and railroads. The Postal Service is the only federal agency that is also a corporate entity. Despite the rare mishap, we remain the envy of global mail services."

Monkey-King, "Is that so? Pray, enlighten me."

Tyler, "Wherever people live—even deep forests or desolate plains—mail reaches them. 200,000 postal carriers work six days a week, through wind and rain. Look at this hall—shelves piled with parcels, tape stations, standardized boxes—all free, all for the people. By the way, the US Postal Service even represents the federal government in processing passports!"

Monkey-King (nodding), "I've seen it myself. Your service is genuine and dependable. But I also heard postage rates go up every other year—Is that true?"

Tyler smirked as he pointed at a man in the distance.

"Yes, and that's because of people like him."

Monkey-King looked around.

A man with Chinese features, dressed neatly in a suit, was tucking free tape into his pocket after sealing his package.

Monkey-King's face twisted in shame. He stormed over:

> "You disgrace! What lowly back-alley clan spawned you? Making us Chinese look bad out here!"

The man jumped, dropping his package as it burst open. Ginseng, fish oil, and all the usual health products spill onto the floor.

> Man (muttering while picking up his staff from the floor): "Oh, my god. I cannot believe my eyes. Monkey-King, Monkey-King is here! What, now even immortals have gone abroad? Hi, the Invincible god,

this is just a tape, man! Americans waste so much of it—this isn't a big deal."

Tyler laughed at the scene.

Seeing Monkey-King still fuming, he tugged at his sleeve:

"Leave him here. Let it go. Our mission is to find the bone, remember?"

They went to see the Postmaster General, a man in a fine wool suit, lounging in a leather chair with his feet on the desk.

After hearing their story, he frowned:

"The parcel was damaged, and you've been compensated. So, what else can we do? Why do you come back? It's just... a piece of bone. Why not replace it with a prosthetic one?"

The Great Mail Heist

Monkey-King had heard enough and became furious, "My brother lost real flesh and bone, not some trinket you can price in silver!"

He kicked the desk over with a roar, sending papers and pens flying, and shouted:

"You're the head of the post office, and you let mail go missing? That's on you! Take me to search now—or I'll knock your head off your neck!"

The postmaster, who had never seen anyone with such thunderous energy, trembled, grabbed a ring of keys, and hurriedly led Monkey-King and Tyler into the parcel sorting facility.

Inside, packages piled up like mountains. Conveyor belts snaked across the room—packages zooming back and forth, workers rushing to and from.

Postmaster (humble panting), "Mr. Pigsy is well-known here in New York City. He plays that iron rake of his. It's only right that I help. I will do my best to locate his missing bone. But these days, mail volume has exploded tremendously. We hired a thousand more hands, and we're still drowning in packages!"

He indicated a few pristine stacks of shiny boxes.

"These packages look luxurious but are actually worthless. Sent cross-country only to be trashed unopened. They are called junk mail! They waste our manpower and clog the system! We don't know how to handle them properly. It delays our...," he said.

America's Trash Mail

Monkey-King felt puzzled.

Tyler stepped in to explain:

"These are mass mailers from businesses, slick catalogs, and product samples. They send them regardless of need, to every address in America. Millions of companies compete to stuff your mailbox. It's basically a national plague."

Monkey-King (raising his eyebrow):

"If this trash clogs your system and wastes resources— why not just ban it?"

Postmaster (sighing):

182

"Here in America, constitutional rights include freedom of the press and mail. We can't ban it. We have to deliver it. Every household then tosses it straight into the bin and moves on. A great waste of paper and fuel."

He pointed out the window, "See those?"

"Those are our commercial mail cannons—used exclusively for launching junk mail from each business corporation." The Postmaster continued.

Monkey-King looked out the window.

Across an open field stood fifty gleaming silver cannons, each as wide as a dining table, labeled with the names of various U.S. cities.

Strong workers in blue uniforms shoveled stacks of shiny envelopes into the barrels. Then,

"BOOM!"

The ground shook as a salvo of advertisements exploded into the sky, scattering like blossoms in springtime. There goes the junk mail all over the land — a true display of American scale and industrial pride.

Monkey-King watched in amazement with his mouth open.

"Heaven help us... such grandeur. What absurdity for spam mail." He said.

A Poem in Witness in Funny Melody

Cannon roars, Boom, Boom!

Junk mail flies skyward across the land,
A wasteful storm no one had planned.
Billions squandered, forests aching sore,
Yet no one pauses—what's it for?

Each village, town, and distant hamlet
Receives dull ads, no one cares to scan them.
Straight to the trash goes every brand,
A madness sweeping through the land.

Cannon roars, Boom, Boom!

In the Warehouse

The Postmaster led them to a locked storage room.

"These are all unclaimed or misrouted items," he said. "I'll assign a few staff to sort through them during the day until tomorrow; all my personnel are deployed. I hope the Great Monkey-King can understand my sincerity."

Monkey-King, "Why don't you take a break? I'll search for it myself."

The postmaster turned pale.

"Please, no! You might not realize that U.S. postal law strictly protects privacy. I can't let you stay here alone. If I let you handle a private parcel and someone files a lawsuit, I could lose my job... maybe even get arrested! I have children to feed at home, sir. Please, just spare me!"

The Monkey Has a Plan

Monkey-King laughed.

"Relax. I won't put you in trouble. Nor will you need to trouble yourself tomorrow."

With that, he turned and left with the group. But, dear reader, Monkey-King hadn't given up, far from it.

Once outside, he slipped away from the others, cast an invisibility spell, and snuck back into the facility.

Seeing the area too busy to move freely for a stranger, he plucked a clump of hair from behind his ear, blew a breath of magic on it—poof! It turned into a swarm of sleep bugs[26] that went straight to the mailroom workers. In moments, everyone inside the postal building began yawning. One by one, they collapsed—deep in enchanted slumber.

Monkey-King sneaked into the storage room. From his robe, he pulled out more hairs and transformed them into a dozen clever little monkeys.

The mini-monkeys squealed with glee and immediately carried orders from Monkey-King and began tearing through the warehouse, overturning boxes, sniffing through crates. The whole place was turned into a bustling working site.

Will Monkey-King find Pigsy's lost limb?
Will justice be delivered to the U.S. postal system?

Let's find out in the next chapter.

---

[26] These sleeping bugs, land on people and make them fall asleep immediately.

Figure 15 Unfolding the bundle, he burst into delighted laughter, for inside lay a small rice pot, a gas stove, cabbage, etc Monkey-King, his belly rumbling with hunger, seized the honeyed cakes and fruits to chew upon, praising between bites. The produce of China truly bears the flavor of "original essence" and "authentic taste."

Chapter 14: Monkey-King Morphs into a Mouse Meeting, Pigsy Fails the Medical Bill

We left off with Monkey-King and his monkey squad turning the post office warehouse upside down. Suddenly, a flurry of squeaks and chatter came from the corner. Monkey-King looked over.

The Bone Thieves Gathering

There by the wall: a group of rats, about two dozen, each half a foot long, standing, crouching, twitching, tail-flicking. One rat stood on a stone in the center, gesturing with its paws like a general giving orders.

> Monkey-King (thinking): "Well now! These American rats sure eat well—look at that one, built like a cat. Let's see what they're up to."

With his fist raised, Monkey-King disguised his monkey form, then transformed into a rat, slipping smoothly with the rat crowd. He scurried into the group just as their leader rat squeaked out:

> "Yesterday, we worked together and snatched Pigsy's arm bone from a mail conveyor — what a great catch!

> "This isn't just any old scrap of bone, my friend. Cats run away from it for some mysterious reason. Snakes go around it. It's a sacred relic!

> "We'll cut this bone into pieces and craft some lovely neck charms for ourselves. That way, we can go outside without fear—what a life we'll have!"

The rats cheered enthusiastically, jumping and squeaking with joy.

Hearing this, Monkey-King thought to himself, "Well, well, I never imagined that Pigsy's bones have this magic power."

He then stifled a snort and sharply whistled.

Monkey-King (aloud, slyly):
"But if Pigsy is as powerful and vengeful as people say, he probably won't let this go easily. What if he comes looking for his missing limb—are we all doomed?"

The rat leader flicked his whiskers and said:

"Pigsy's at the hospital, enjoying time with his wife Cuilan by his bedside.

"He is lazy and loves food. In just a few days, he's already bloated like a dumpling. His arms and legs are chunky. His movement is so slow that he can't even catch a flea these days. No need to worry!"

Monkey-King pushed further:

"Well, sure, but what about Monkey-King, his monkey brother? He's got magic, a golden stick, and a temper like a wildfire. Wouldn't it be safer to give the bone back and call it even? We will make friends with Monkey-King!"

That drew a scornful squeak from the rat leader.

He said, "Bah! Stop listening to this little punk. That monkey only knows brute strength, swinging sticks, and playing tough.

"He's no match for our king, Mickey Mouse, master of subtlety and charm! Our King Mickey Mouse is known to overcome 'rigidity' with 'flexibility'. He is the champion to conquer 'hardness' with 'softness'.[27]

"Mickey defeats enemies without lifting even a paw—with jokes and mischief, not muscles." That monkey is a foolish foe. He poses no real challenge. "

A rat wandered around Monkey-King, sniffing with suspicion, and reported:

"This fellow has a strange smell. Oh, it's like the urinating scent of a monkey, and his fur isn't like ours. Strange—could he be Monkey-King in disguise?!"

All rats were frightened, but before they could react, Monkey-King somersaulted and transformed into a spotted wildcat—fur like gold, eyes like lanterns, fangs clicking like castanets.

The rats screamed, "AIIIIIEEEE!" and bolted in all directions.
Even the leader dived behind the very stone he'd been standing on.

Monkey-King narrowed his eyes at the sight.

Monkey-King (smirking), "Well, look at that. The 'stone' turns out to be Pigsy's arm bone after all!"

---

[27] Use soft power to battle 'hardness' is highly regarded in Chinese philosophical literature.

He picked up the bone with a grin, reverted to his usual self, and headed back to the hospital, leaving behind a trail of panicked rat squeals.

Monkey vs. Mouse – A Rivalry for the Ages

Readers may recognize that if Monkey-King is the most remarkable monkey of all time, then Mickey Mouse is undoubtedly the most exceptional mouse. Monkey-King wins through strength. Mickey wins through charm. Monkey-King instills fear with a pole as a weapon and a glare; the other, Mickey, disarms with giggles and jests. When these two kings one day cross paths—Monkey-King versus the Mouse King—the showdown will become legendary.

But that, dear readers, is a story for another chapter.

Back at the Hospital

Monkey-King triumphantly returned just as Pigsy and the others were on the verge, watching the door anxiously and pacing. Dr. Tyler nodded and took the arm bone to begin work on Pigsy.

"Bang, Bang." Dr. Tyler used a shining hammer to reattach Pigsy's arm.

Of course, Pigsy wailed all the way.

Pigsy (howling):
"AYY-YO! AYY-YO! That hurts!"

His wife, Cuilan, rolled her eyes and rubbed his back to comfort him. "What're you yelling for? Back on the farm, when folks nail horseshoes, the horses don't make this much fuss!"

Pigsy (groaning), "What kind of comparison is that? When they neuter pigs in the village, it's never quiet. This is me we're talking about! If I don't say it hurts, how will the doctor know? He might strike harder than necessary."

Monkey-King and the nurses silenced their laughter.

Dr. Tylor smiled. A few clinks and clanks later, it was installed—seamless as before, like fine carpentry.

Pigsy stood up, stretched, and his new arm felt as good as ever. He rubbed his belly.

"This hospital stay is worth it. It's really something; I've gained three inches of belly fat in just two days!" He declared.

He clapped Tyler on the shoulder:

"Come visit our martial arts school sometime. My wife will make you a proper home-cooked meal."

Tyler smiled again, nodded, and waved for the nurses to start Pigsy's discharge paperwork. Then he grabbed his tools and jerked away in a hurry.

Monkey-King watched him vanish.

Monkey-King (thinking): "That was awfully quick… didn't even say goodbye yet. Strange."

Just then, three nurses walked in, each carrying a large stack of invoices.

Monkey-King (alarmed), "Wua-oh. Looks like Dr. Tyler slipped out on purpose... and left us to deal with the bill collectors."

The First Bill: Check-Up Shock

A tall, slim nurse stepped forward, stern-faced as if marching into battle. She held up the bill and spoke in a solemn voice:

"Patient underwent an examination of ears, nose, throat, eyes, teeth, tongue, hair, and mouth.

Fee: 200 taels of fine silver. Now pay up!"

Pigsy nearly choked. For a basic check-up, the fee was two-thirds of his monthly income.

Pigsy (grumbling):
"I train all month in my martial arts school—swinging rakes, throwing punches, sweating my soul out—and only make 100 taels a day. How's this worth two hundred? And in *fine* silver, too?"

The nurse didn't reply. She calmly took down the martial arts school's bank account number, made Pigsy sign off on 200 taels, and stepped back.

The Second Bill: Bed, Food, and Weight Gain

Just as that matter was settled, a short, plump nurse waddled in with another bill, reciting:

"Patient selected two striped hospital gowns—100 taels.
Lodging, two days—200 taels.

Meals, two days—200 taels.
Weight gain, 200 pounds—200 taels.

Discount of 50 taels.

Grand total: 650 taels of fine silver. Now pay up!"

Pigsy's eyes bulged, and he grew nervous, "I've only got three hundred taels left! Even if I gave it all to you, I'd still be three hundred short! Where am I supposed to find the rest?"

Monkey-King (stepping in), "I've been working for a month at the horse ranch—saved up exactly 300 taels. You can take that too… but we're still short fifty."

As the old saying goes, "When a man's broke, his spirit shrinks like a dying flame."
Even heroes like Monkey-King and Pigsy, at this moment, looked deflated and beaten.

Cuilan, watching them both pale and speechless, quickly untied her bundled bag, pulled out 50 taels, and handed them over.

She whispered to the nurse.

Cuilan (pleading), "This was our travel money for the journey home. We've given it all. Please, is there any way to lower the fee?"

But the nurse said nothing; her face was as cold as porcelain. She took the money, copied the account numbers, and made both men sign for 600 taels.

The Final Blow: Surgical Charges

Then came a third nurse, skin pale and neat like fresh printer paper. She sang:

"Bone removal fee—5,000 taels.
Straightening and reassembly—5,000 taels.
Reinstallation—5,000 taels.

Grand total: 15,000 taels of fine silver. Pay immediately."

The nervous Pigsy heard this and nearly fainted.

Pigsy (collapsing):
"Fifteen thousand?! Are you trying to kill me, or cure me?!"

Cuilan rushed to prop him up.

Cuilan, "My dear, you've been in America for a while—do you have any savings?"

Pigsy (sighing), "I still have 10,000 taels in Citibank. That's all I've got. My life savings! I was going to use it to buy land and build us a home."

Cuilan (resolute), "Well, debts must be paid. Dreams can wait. We're still short 5,000 taels. Can we... pay on credit?"

The nurse replied icily:

"Sure. But remind you that credit is charged 50 taels of interest every two weeks, settled biweekly."

Without further discussion, she had Pigsy transfer his entire Citibank account.

Cuilan watched her husband go from modest wealth to total bankruptcy in an instant—and now, they're drowning in debt with no relief in sight. She burst into tears.

Pigsy, reflecting on all his labor in this foreign land, now all lost in just one hospital stay, let out a deep, heartbroken sigh or roar instead.

Even a few nearby janitors and assistants, watching this sad pair so helpless and exhausted, wiped away tears themselves. The room fell silent—just sniffles and sorrow.

A Poem Bears Witness:

> *"The hospital's lion mouth consumes,*
> *Devours the flesh, leaves not a bone.*
> *Pity the kind-hearted immigrant pair—*
> *Lost in debt, they weep alone."*

A song for the sorrow,

> *Land of the Free, yet fears are fresh.*
> *Headache, stomach ache, never to the hospital queue.*
>
> *So many folks… silently endure,*
> *Between life and death, teeth clenched of the poor—*
> *Wrong, wrong, wrong!*
>
> *Immigrant dream, will it ever come true?*
> *Body breaks down, hopes break too.*
>
> *So many people save every dime,*
> *Working through pain, all savings to the hospital wards—*
> *No, no, no!*

195

Monkey-King Had Enough

Monkey-King, hearing all the sobbing in the room and corridor, couldn't take it anymore.

He stopped the nurses from leaving.

Monkey-King (furious), "What kind of blasted hospital is this?! Prices are sky high—how's any regular person supposed to afford them?! Get me Dr. Tyler—now! The Great Sage has words for him!"

Without waiting, he took the bills from their hands, tore them into confetti, and scattered the shreds on the floor.

The nurses screamed and ran in panic, calling for Dr. Tyler and summoning two security guards to flank him.

Monkey-King pointed at Dr. Tyler, his voice raging with fury.

Monkey-King, "These outrageous medical fees! It's all because of your unnecessary tests. My brother's injury is in his arm, yet you check his ears, hair, temperature, blood pressure, eyes, and nose—what do those have to do with a broken bone? You're just draining us with fancy excuses!"

Dr. Tyler raised his hands, trying to soothe him.

Dr. Tyler (hastily), "Please, Great Sage, calm yourself—I understand your concerns. But you must realize, here in the United States, even the tiniest medical mistake can lead to lawsuits worth millions.

"We must be prepared. Trial lawyers make a living digging through treatment records for even the slightest flaw to pin on us. We do all these extra checks not because they're essential—but because we can't afford to leave anything out.

"This isn't your Celestial Empire, where what can be skipped is skipped. This is America — if it can be billed, it will be billed."

Monkey-King, "Don't tell me you're just afraid of lawsuits. The real reason is profit! You charged 10,000 taels for setting one broken bone. Why?"

Dr. Tyler, "Simple economics. In your land, doctors see hundreds of patients daily—thin profits spread wide and collected. Here, there are a few patients. A doctor may see only three or five patients a day. To keep the lights on, to feed the nurses, to fund this grand building—we must charge more.

You may not like the number, but every 10,000 taels has its justification. If you don't have the money, go and borrow. Many lenders are waiting to jump in. Don't waste time arguing—it won't help you."

A Sudden Discovery

While Monkey-King and Tyler argued, Cuilan observed something odd.

She pointed out a few patients walking out of the hospital without paying a single coin—no bills, no fuss.

Pigsy erupted in anger. He yanked Tyler's sleeve and yelled, "That woman left without paying! She must be your favorite piece! You cover her costs and squeeze mine? Are you paying her debt with my silver taels?!"

Security guards rushed over and pulled Pigsy back, scolding him, "Another outburst, and we'll call the cops for physical aggression. No body language, please, sir!"

Tyler Explains the System

Dr. Tyler (calmly), "That woman has health insurance. The bill was sent to her insurance provider— she pays nothing. If you had insurance, you could do the same."

Seeing their confusion, he elaborated, "In America, insurance is the key. There's health insurance and life insurance. You pay a premium while you're healthy, and when you fall ill, the company pays the bill. Life insurance, you pay while you're alive, and after death, your family gets the payout—so your loved ones don't suffer when you're gone."

Cuilan, "Can I buy insurance too?"

Dr. Tyler (shaking his head), "Rushing to buy at the last second? I fear it's too late. But, perhaps, there's still a way…"

Tyler called Monkey-King aside and whispered something into his ear.

Monkey-King's face lit up. He quickly shared the plan with Pigsy and Cuilan, and their mood suddenly brightened. The trio broke into smiles, the gloom lifting like morning fog.

A Secret Revealed to the Reader

Now, dear reader, do you understand why American hospitals are so eager to help patients "find money"?

Because hospital expenses are massive, and unpaid debts give administrators headaches. If a broke patient defaults, there's little they can do. Even throwing someone in jail won't recoup the cash. And so, when a patient can't pay, the hospital panics more than the patient does!

Hence, many hospitals have partnerships with charities, churches, relief funds, and donation networks to help indigent patients survive the system.

But here's the key. Before any help is given, the hospital will always ask, *"Do you have your own way to make money?"*

And how could Dr. Tyler not know that Monkey-King and Pigsy are not at all broke foreigners? Their powers could shift mountains and reverse rivers—money was never beyond their reach. They just needed someone to point them in the right direction.

What did Dr. Tyler whisper?
How will Monkey-King get them out of debt?
What twist awaits our weary trio next?

Tune in to the next chapter to find out!

Figure 16 Seeing her husband stripped of every coin in an instant and burdened with towering debts that might never be repaid, Cuilan could not help but break into bitter tears.

Chapter 15: Monkey-King's Insurance Charm, The Registry of Hells

By now, Dr. Tyler, fully aware that Pigsy had no money to settle his bill, whispered a suggestion to Monkey-King.

Dr. Tyler, "This land, America, is paved with gold, if only you know where to scoop it up. Insurance and banking are the surest ways to riches. Why not try your hand at that?"

Monkey-King frowned. He said, "I've heard that selling insurance requires a silver tongue and endless smooth-talking. You have to roam around, charm folks, and butter them up. That doesn't fit my personality, and besides, I'm new here—don't know the language or the customs. It doesn't seem easy."

Dr. Tyler smiled, "Come now, don't be modest. You've got deep connections with King Yama himself, who rules the hells. Selling life insurance should be child's play for you!"

At that moment, realization hit Monkey-King. He clapped his hands in delight, praising the idea.

Dr. Tyler, "As for Pigsy's debt, don't worry, we can delay the payment. Tonight, go home and rest. Tomorrow on the hospital lawn, there will be a massive insurance expo—a cutthroat battlefield of salespeople and companies. That's your stage to shine."

So Monkey-King and his crew packed up and went back to their martial arts school for the night.

The Great Insurance Expo

At dawn the next day, crowds already swarmed across the hospital's expansive lawn. Red, blue, green, and yellow banners fluttered overhead, some tall, some short. Dozens of insurance companies had gathered to compete for customers, eager to establish dominance.

Tents stood tall, booths stretched in long rows, and tables were clean and covered. Salespeople, men and women alike, wore bright smiles and polished shoes. Some were dressed in suits and ties, others in elegant dresses.

Dear reader, understand this: the American insurance industry is unrivaled. From forests and mines to earrings and teacups, anything of value can be insured.

- House insurance

- Car insurance

- Life insurance

- Medical insurance

- Any new ideas (intellectual property insurance)

You name it — they insure it.

Credit card fraud? Insurance!
Food poisoning at your restaurant? Insurance!
Tourist scratched by a monkey? Insurance!
Lost your job? Insurance!

Personal injuries, of course, are covered. Even the racing horse's legs!

You find it, they insure it.

Truly, there is no object too small, no event too obscure—from mosquito bites to global disasters, everything can be insured.

As a result, millions are employed in the field, and the industry has grown so large that it now stands as one of the pillars of the American economy, shoulder to shoulder with the auto industry and agriculture.

Monkey-King woke up early, washed up, and headed to the hospital lawn with Adam. Pigsy stayed behind, teaching students, conducting drills, and watching over the school.

Monkey-King and Adam mingled with the crowd, wide-eyed and cautious. Monkey-King whispered, "Let's not rush in. I want to observe first—learn how these folks swindle so sweetly."

The Insurance Booth Performer

Soon, they noticed a burly salesman, towering above the crowd, arms flailing dramatically, his voice booming:

"Got a house? Listen well to this! It may stand firm today, but one blaze and it's all gone. Didn't you see that massive racetrack in New York last week? Went up in flames, 'Puff', gone in minutes, just like that!"

He snapped his fingers for effect, and the crowd leaned in as he continued.

"Got real estate? Think twice! Just the other day, a flood in the Midwest swallowed thousands of acres! Water shows no mercy!

"Fires and floods make no friends in this world; everywhere, it's the same!

"Tornadoes? They go where they please! I saw a whole building lifted into the air like a feather. This land of ours is a land of cyclones. How will you escape them?"

Then he pointed dramatically at the sky.

"Early this year, scientists warned of a meteor heading for Earth—a thousand times more powerful than a nuclear bomb! Not the end of the world yet, but it's close!"

The crowd gasped, pale and trembling.

Then, softening his tone and flashing a smile, he concluded:

"Thank heavens for my Universal Property & Real Estate Insurance Corp. We cover everything— from meteors overhead to floods and fires below. Guaranteed safety. Tenfold compensation if we fail to pay within 10 days."

The people breathed a sigh of relief and rushed to sign up with Universal Property. Millions of dollars go that way in a minute.

Monkey-King smiled softly:

"What a silver tongue! He transformed their mild concern into mortal terror, then offered salvation. Clever logic! I can't compete with that."

Adam nodded:

"The American market thrives on persuasion. After centuries of capitalism, even housewives and toddlers here can pitch like professionals.

"If you can't master this craft, you're beaten before the battle begins. How can you sell insurance without a killer pitch?

They moved to another booth where two company reps had taken off their suits and put on ancient-style armor—one with a blue shield, the other with a blue spear.

They engaged in mock combat, clashing shields with spears, moving smoothly as a pair.

A crowd quickly formed, fascinated by their performance, and cheered every move.

Then one rep stepped forward, raising the blue shield, and shouted:

"We all eat and drink—strong as bulls, tough as boars—but who among us hasn't ever fallen ill? Sickness spares no one! Just look at Pigsy from the Eastern Martial School, the Master of Rake in TV these days—once full of life, now buried in debt after just two nights in the hospital!

"We at Blue Shield Health Insurance don't just feel sorry for you — we urge you to take action and join. Medical costs keep rising, and illness lurks like a beast in the dark. Who can walk with peace of mind without our coverage? No one!

"We are the #1 in America—solid as a rock, firm and tough as this shield!"

He banged it for effect. The crowd roared.

A woman in the crowd raised a concern, "Blue Shield may be good, but people say you can only see approved doctors in your network, which is very inconvenient. And sick folks must pay extra premiums to join. I know other companies that don't have these limits."

The Blue Shield representative clapped and laughed heartily:

"Where in the world is there such a thing as a free lunch? Why do we restrict your choice of doctors? To keep costs low and prevent shady quacks from inflating prices! All our approved doctors aren't just professionals; they're miracle workers too.

"And why do we restrict people with pre-existing conditions? Because some folks game the system—joining when they're sick, then leaving when they're cured. Look at that Pigsy, who owes the hospital 10,000 silver taels. Should we just let him join now and burden everyone else?

He swept his gaze across the crowd and continued:

"And you wonder why Blue Shield leads the pack? Take measles and smallpox, shingles, deadly as they are, most companies cover them only once per lifetime. But us? An unlimited number of claims. Get sick again with measles? We'll cover it again!"[28]

The audience nodded in agreement.

The rep continued, as if reciting a creed:

---

[28] These medical conditions are rare due to vaccines; they typically occur only once in people.

"Once, only the wealthy could afford insurance. But today, Blue Shield introduces a People's Health Plan—low premiums, open to everyone. Don't wait! Join now! Don't be like that Pigsy, who waited too long and now suffers for it!"

Immediately, people started pulling out their wallets and rushing to sign up. Millions of dollars flowed in as well.

Monkey-King Reacts

Monkey-King scowled:

"My brother Pigsy might be a little greedy, but since walking the path of Buddha, he's been kind to everyone. This fellow's public shaming is outrageous! Just you wait—I'll call Pigsy over and give that guy a taste of his rake!"

Adam gently intervened:

"I don't think the Blue Shield rep meant any real offense—he was just using Pigsy, a well-known celebrity, as an example for his business. Now that Pigsy's a public figure, he'll have to get used to both praise and criticism. These street-level sales talks may sound crude, but they're not malicious.

"Besides, even though insurance companies rake in the cash, they deal with plenty of tricksters and fraudsters. The Blue Shield guy's good at reading people and calculating risk—that's how they stay afloat. If you trust everyone as honest as you do… how will you ever sell insurance? You'll just lose your shirt."

The Jeep Insurance Extravaganza

The two walked over to another large booth, where colorful banners fluttered, and tables were topped with glossy brochures and stuffed animals. A friendly-looking salesperson stood nearby, constantly handing out flyers and toys to passersby.

On a raised platform, a brand-new convertible Jeep stood open to anyone who wanted to hop in and try the seats.

In front of the Jeep, several young women in stylish outfits sang and danced, microphones in hand, swaying their hips to an exotic rhythm. The crowd thickened, bouncing and moving along with the music like waves.

They sang:

> *"I came from the desert,*
> *Where the sands blow wild,*
> *But I rode home in this Jeep.*
>
> *I came from the plateau,*
> *Where snow and wind bite,*
> *But I rode home in this Jeep.*
>
> *I came from the wasteland,*
> *Where the roads are ravines,*
> *But I rode home in this Jeep.*
>
> *A thousand dangers I've passed,*
> *All gone, all gone—thanks to Jeep Vehicle*
> *Insurance!"*

As the song ended, a company rep shouted:

"Anyone who signs up for Jeep Vehicle Insurance today will be entered into our Jeep Lottery—you could drive this Jeep home today!

"No tricks! No lies! Only cannot promise the beauty…" The crowd laughed.

Monkey-King's Inspiration

Monkey-King was stirred:

"What a beautiful song. It touches my heart too! I traveled across the endless desert plains. On my journey to India, we passed countless towns, but I don't remember the names of any of them. However, I still recall the sight of 'lone smoke rising straight upward in the desert'… unforgettable."

Adam nodded:

"Exactly the effect they aim for. The song and dance draw you in emotionally, linking the Jeep to rugged terrain and man's courage and freedom. The subliminal message? With your Jeep fully insured, you have peace of mind and can go anywhere without fear.

"The Jeep symbolizes rugged masculine adventure, which draws attractive women to dance beside it. Insurance marketing relies heavily on psychology and persuasion. Wukong, Mr. Monkey-King, still think you can do better? Do you still believe you can outshine them?"

Monkey-King grinned:

"Their little tricks? Child's play! Want to see how it's done? Follow me."

Monkey-King's Grand Entrance

He led Adam to the very center of the lawn.

With a sudden breath, Monkey-King blew a gust of celestial wind—whoosh! Everything blew into the air. Papers scattered, picnic cloths fluttered, and visitors hurried to gather their belongings, leaving an open space.

Monkey-King raised his Golden-Hooped pole, spinning it until it gleamed gold in every direction. The crowd stepped back in awe, forming a large circle.

With a thunderous slam, he struck the ground.

Baang!

Suddenly, a grand stage burst from the earth, towering into the sky. Silver light shimmered across its surface. Colorful flags sprouted from all sides, and the 50-foot-high light poles gleamed overhead as the music began.

Monkey-King pointed at the sky.

The clouds parted, and brightly colored birds soared down from above, holding a hundred-foot-long blue banner in their beaks.

The white clouds twisted into words, forming glowing letters in the sky:

"Monkey-King Life Insurance"

The ribbons fluttered, and the banner gently unfurled, connecting sky to earth as the glowing banner hung above the stage.

People rushed over, stunned and speechless, forming a vast crowd, a sea of heads. And the entire audience was in awe.

Adam clapped and cheered:

"Magnificent spectacle indeed! Still, the people of America are often captivated by visual marvels… Go ahead, but when it comes to actual buying, they hesitate."

Monkey-King said nothing. With a sharp whistle, a troupe of Texas cowboys sprang up onto the stage—wide-brimmed hats atop their heads, long whips in hand, leaping and stomping to the music, full of vigor and might.

A song began:

"Herding cattle on open plains—
To build a home, a man must be brave.

Whips cracking, songs soaring—
With a wife and child, a man must be brave.

Campfires roaring against the sky—
Together, in peace, a man must be brave.

Let all else be cast aside—
Life insurance eases every man's burden."

Monkey-King found a cowboy hat, grabbed a whip, and joined the dancers on stage, twirling and stomping. The crowd burst into laughter. Among them, many sturdy men stepped forward to ask about the insurance. They are family men, providers, and pillars of their households.

Why is that? Though feminism may seem loud in America, deep down in the heart, the old ways still linger—men earn, women tend to the home. If a man falls, who cares for his family? Tie life insurance to pride and duty, and men will rush to buy it.

Adam said thoughtfully:

"The cowboy style is rough and bold, yet it shows love for home and kin—quite touching indeed. But its appeal is too narrow—only a certain kind of folks respond. It won't bring in big money."

Hearing what Adam said, desperate Monkey-King gave another sharp whistle. The cowboys vanished, and suddenly a deep, eerie brass blast echoed. The drums slowed, becoming slow and haunting, as a group of ghosts and demons swarmed the stage— green faces, fangs bared, writhing and leaping in sinister fashion.

A chant rang out:

"A life is fleeting like an ant's—
Will you live or die? Who can say?

You live, I die; I live, you die—
Are you in this world or the next? Who can
say?"

The audience, swaying to the rhythm, started to feel a sense of impermanence. Murmurs turned into tears.

Suddenly, the horns blared again. A line of Ox-Heads and Horse-Faces, underworld officers, stepped onto the stage, escorting a crimson-robed Judge of Death, the Yama, King of Hells.[29]

He bowed to Monkey-King:

"We heard the Great Sage called for us. What is your wish?"

Monkey-King declared:

"Today, I establish this Life Insurance Company to help raise funds for Pigsy's hospital bills. I am about to let all those enrolled in my insurance have their lifespan extended by 70 years! You must assist in this."

Yama King bowed. Monkey-King then cracked his whip three times and turned to the crowd:

"My insurance is honored in Heaven and in Hell, too! Enrollees gain 70 extra years of life! At the century mark, fate will be reconsidered based on one's deeds. Premium: 200 silver taels total—just two taels per year!"

The audience was bewildered, unsure whether to believe.

Monkey-King pointed at the crimson-robed Yama:

"This is none other than King Yama, ruler of the Underworld, keeper of the Book of Life and Death. Your fate is already written—just 70 or 80 years if

---

[29] Yama, the King of Hell's movement is often accompanied by his servants, Ox-Heads and House-Faces of the underworld, according to Chinese literature.

you're lucky. Why not buy some extra years while you still can?"

As his words landed, an elderly man, trembling and leaning on his family relatives, stepped forward to enroll. Monkey-King collected the silver.

King Yama quickly flipped through his registry book:

"Your life was scheduled to end next month.
I now extend it by 70 more years."

With a stroke of his red brush, he amended the book. Instantly, the old man stood upright and lively, his back straight, energy restored—his white hair turned black like a child's.

The crowd was amazed, and even Adam became totally flabbergasted.

More and more came forward—young and old, men and women, all lining up to enroll. Those without silver rushed to banks to fetch dollars. Word spread far and wide, drawing thousands from every direction.

Even patients from the hospital came hobbling and limping, dragging IV poles, rushing to join the line.

The crowd almost crushed King Yama.

Monkey-King quickly ordered Ox-Heads and Horse-Faces to open several more enrollment lines, while a few little guys from the underworld with Yama maintained order. Monkey-King and Adam sat at the table, counting the silver, too busy even to laugh.

High atop the hospital roof, Doctor Taylor peered through the window—and smiled.

214

To find out how Monkey-King and Pigsy spend their newfound fortune, tune in to the next chapter.

Figure 17 As soon as the words landed, an elderly person, trembling and unsteady, was assisted forward by their family to sign up for insurance.

Chapter 16: Monkey-King Hates Paying Taxes, Teacher Rejoices at the Donation

After enlisting King Yama to co-manage a life insurance operation, Monkey-King quickly struck gold. In just the time it took to eat a meal, they had gathered a large amount of silver dollars. But King Yama, being a busy bureaucrat of the underworld, couldn't stay long. He stirred up a cold infernal breeze, said farewell to Monkey-King, and left with Ox-Head and Horse-Face for the netherworld.

Celebration at the Martial Arts School

Seeing the piles of silver dollars, Monkey-King took some to pay for Pigsy's hospital bills. Afterwards, he and Adam called in several trucks to transport the coins back to their martial arts school. The trip was lively and full of excitement, as if they were celebrating a victory parade.

Back at the school, the sight of the silver stunned Pigsy and the others. Delighted, they held a grand banquet in traditional Chinese fashion, distributing rewards based on merit. Cuilan, Pigsy's wife, busily served food and drinks, glowing with excitement. Despite the chaos, her enthusiasm was obvious—she was now eager to secure her green card; she was sure her village's best sisters would be jealous but happy for her.

An Unexpected Visit from the IRS

Shortly after noon the next day, Monkey-King and Pigsy returned from a walk to find several well-dressed Americans, clearly IRS agents and tax agency professionals, sitting in the main hall.

Adam was talking with a few of them and quickly approached the returning duo.

"The federal tax agents are here but just left," Adam explained. "They were here asking about the insurance proceeds and pressing for tax payments. Next time they come, we'll need to be prepared."

Pigsy exploded, "I was in the hospital, broke and desperate, and the government didn't lift a finger to help! And now they want taxes? You think this money came easy? Next time they show up, I'll flatten them with my rake!"

Monkey-King added indignantly, "The silver dollars aren't even warm in my hands, and already they're pounding on my door? Is this IRS out to get me? I'm the Great Sage Equal to Heaven! I don't fall under earthly jurisdiction, so why should I pay their blasted taxes?"

Adam hurriedly stepped in, "Please, Immortals, hear me out. The United States might appear wealthy on the surface, but in reality, it's spending beyond its means. Huge government expenses—healthcare, education, social welfare—drain its coffers. On top of that, constant wars and foreign aid have made it borrow from the future for years.

"That's why taxation is the top priority for every government, more urgent than diplomacy or national defense. Every American, regardless of background, must face two certainties: you will die, and you will pay taxes. Federal tax law affects everyone, from the President down to the common person. Forgive my bluntness, but even Guanyin or the Buddha wouldn't be exempt if they lived in the U.S."

Monkey-King Plans to Conceal the Money

Monkey-King smirked, "I've got more than enough tricks. I'll hide my money somewhere the IRS will never find it. When they come asking, I'll say it all went toward Pigsy's medical bills—nothing left."

Pigsy clapped. "Great idea, Monkey Brother! I'll go dig a hole out back in the yard. With silver coins buried, we won't fear famine or illness—we'll always have something to fall back on!" And off he went with his iron rake.

Adam chuckled, "Such tricks? Already reported to the IRS. Anyone who bought your insurance will need to declare it when seeking medical treatment or damages. IRS agents might not have divine powers, but they have a keen nose for money. They go everywhere, sniffing out the slightest clue. With all the noise from yesterday's event, which drew in so many people, how could this have escaped their notice?"

He went on, "The U.S. tax system is over 200 years old, airtight, and unforgiving. Try hiding now, and you'll only face double penalties later. Don't say I didn't warn you."

"You think with so many taxpayers, the IRS can't keep track?" Adam continued. "Other departments may be lazy, but the IRS is thorough and relentless; nothing escapes their scrutiny. That's for sure. Unless you have internal old boy connections, which I doubt you have."

Monkey-King sighed, "We worked hard for those silver dollars. To hand it over for nothing—it's hard to swallow. I doubt Americans will let it go easily. You're from here—got any smart solutions?"

"Now you're talking," Adam nodded. "You're a renowned Buddhist disciple—how could you stoop to the level of shady immigrants dodging taxes? Everyone wants to pay less, but it must be done legally. That's why there are thousands of private tax service agencies in America, skilled in navigating the tax code and finding loopholes.

"IRS agents, no matter how aggressive, must operate within the law. They may be sneaky internally, but they need to appear legitimate on the surface. Why not hire a tax attorney and see what they can do?"

Adam pointed to the gentlemen in suits still in the hall. Don't you Chinese say "the devil raises itself one foot and a Taoist priest raises 10 more? These are people willing to jump in for you. They are tax professionals. Quite a few are trained in Ivy League schools."

Adam pointed toward street vendors outside, saying, "Chinese immigrants work hard to survive. When tax season comes, they often file returns on their own, burning the midnight oil. But without understanding the laws, they end up making up accounts to dodge taxes. They may save a few scraps, but lose out on bigger savings—and once caught, their record is stained forever."

Monkey-King Understands the Stakes

Monkey-King thought to himself, "That makes sense. Back home in China, people love gossiping, exaggerating, and making mountains out of molehills. If word of any shady dealings gets back to my tax story in America, it'll ruin my reputation. For a few coins, is that really worth it?"

So, he turned to Adam and said, "Since there are tax service agencies here, why not try one out? It might save us a headache. Can you point me in the right direction?"

As soon as Monkey-King finished speaking, two of the previously silent gentlemen behind Adam stood up. One of them stepped forward and declared, "I am the chief representative of New York Tax Help, known as 'Count-It-All.' I specialize in assisting small and medium-sized businesses with tax filings. I am skilled in calculating wage expenses and applying federal tax codes to reduce taxable income. I assure you, Mr. Monkey-King, I can ease your tax burdens. Now, show me your business expenses."

Monkey-King was thrilled and replied, "I made good profits selling life insurance, all thanks to King Yama's efforts. I even hired Ox-Head and Horse-Face, along with dozens of little demons to help with the campaign. All of their wages should be counted as expenses, right? King Yama is no ordinary spirit—he wouldn't lift a finger for less than ten million taels of silver! And those little demons? They're not working for mere pocket change either!"

Hearing this, Count-It-All was stunned into silence. Ten million taels as wages? That's bound to trigger the IRS's radar for a tax audit. And those underworld spirits—none of them have legal work permits to claim tax deductions! If discovered, this could ruin his career. Best to quietly step back and avoid this risky business.

Count-It-All shook his head and reluctantly stepped back from taking the business.

The second man now stepped forward, "Wage expenses aren't the most advantageous deduction. According to federal tax law, there's a section on employee training that's even more valuable. Training costs can lower taxes, though the calculation methods are quite nuanced.

"I specialize in this field—I can legally inflate education expenses, and I can also help deduct room, board, and travel. I come from a family of accountants and am known as 'Cover-It-All.' I'd be honored to handle Mr. Sun's tax affairs. Now tell me, how did you learn your skills? You must have attended some trade school, right?"

Monkey-King laughed, "In that case, my cloud-surfing technique should qualify as travel expenses, right? Too bad I didn't pay tuition back when I learned the Seventy-Two Transformations. Could've filed those expenses too."

Cover-It-All hesitated and finally said, "I've never heard of this 'Seventy-Two Transformations' skill, so I can't estimate the tuition. As for flying on clouds, it might eventually fall into the same category as space travel, which is gaining legal acceptance. But until Congress passes a bill, the IRS won't recognize it yet. They remain strict. Without a clear statute, there's little flexibility. I must admit—I can't help with that just yet."

Now, dear reader, you might wonder: Why did both Count-It-All and Cover-It-All hesitate to take Monkey-King's case?

Because the IRS is no ordinary entity, U.S. tax law is precise to the tiniest detail—there's little room for interpretation or ambiguity. The law also clearly states specific penalties, including the amount you'll be fined or the possibility of jail time for tax evasion.

It's a typical story of *"When the Daoist grows a foot taller, the demon grows ten feet stronger."* [30] No taxpayer dares act rashly. Tax agencies, too, tread carefully. They follow the letter of the law and only act when they're confident of a solid legal loophole.

As Monkey-King grew increasingly frustrated with his failed attempts to dodge taxes, Adam said, "Great Sage, there's no need to worry. Under federal tax law, donations to charity or educational

---

[30] Daoists were often hired to fight demons in people's dwellings.

institutions can be deducted from taxable income. As a disciple of the Buddha, why not consider a charitable route? You'd be doing good while lowering your tax burden."

A New Opportunity: Supporting Education

As Adam finished, a group of Americans stepped forward and surrounded Monkey-King. One of them spoke, "We are local teachers, all certified educators. We came together today, hoping to establish a long-term relationship with your insurance company. Our school has long wanted to purchase computers, but lacks the funds. If your company could donate, no matter how much, we would be deeply grateful."

Monkey-King said, "Donating money to education is a blessing for future generations. Much better than paying it all to the IRS demons. That makes me happy indeed. But you are teachers— shouldn't you be focused on quiet study and guiding students? Isn't it inappropriate to be out here publicly asking for money? What if your students saw you—how would that look?"

One of the teachers replied, "In America, there's a big difference between public and private schools. Public schools are funded by the government. However, private schools need to generate their own funds. We all work at private institutions. We're here advocating not for ourselves, but for our students."

Cultural Lessons in Fundraising

Adam smiled at Monkey-King and said, "This is a cultural difference. In America, schools are open about discussing money. There are complete courses dedicated to teaching students how to manage personal finances, save and invest money, balance budgets, and raise funds.

In winter, during the Christmas season, even young students are encouraged to sell holiday gifts to relatives in fundraising contests. In the summer, it's common to see children selling homemade lemonade by the roadside in their communities. Teenagers washing cars and mowing lawns are longstanding traditions. When teachers fundraise, they set an example—leading by doing. It's entirely respectable!

Monkey-King Reflects on the Homeland

Monkey-King replied, "Even in the Celestial Empire, schools have started to expand their fundraising efforts. It's no longer just an American thing."

Adam responded, "I've heard that your fundraising can sometimes seem like coercion. Children often ask their parents for money to meet school quotas, which doesn't help them become more self-reliant. It may appear similar, but in essence, it's quite different."

Monkey-King added, "In the Celestial Empire, many households have only one child. So, parents dote on them, sparing them all hardships. They are fed and clothed without lifting a finger. I myself am not fond of such coddling."

Then he pointed at the pile of silver dollars and told the teachers, "I'll donate all these silver dollars to your school. Saves me the headache of filing taxes, too!"

A Donor Turns into a Hero

The teachers were overjoyed. Readers should understand that it is no coincidence they requested a donation; as soon as they heard Monkey-King's story, they realized they had to try their luck. With the big money coming their way, they told Monkey-King, "With this generous donation, you shall be our next school board chancellor! We'll declare you the Model Educator of Modern America! This is monumental! Why not visit the school now to inspect our operations? I'll call the TV and radio stations to broadcast the event live!"

Monkey-King smiled, "As a follower of the Buddha, I am indifferent to fame or fortune. No need to make a spectacle. Let me see those computers of yours that're supposed to be so precious."

No Free Lunch in America

Adam added from the side, "In America, no one gives away money for nothing. Your donation earns you honor; their school gets funding. That's the secret behind voluntary philanthropy among the wealthy; it's a win-win. As the best philanthropist of the year, you can also move into the political arena and run for government positions! Honor also brings money, too."

Monkey-King began to chant a mantra, preparing to visit the school, and in an instant, a cloud descended from the sky. Monkey-King gestured for the teachers to get on the cloud so they could travel together.

One teacher asked, "Master Pigsy is still in the courtyard digging holes, shall we call him over?"

Monkey-King replied, "No need. He hoards money as if his life depended on it. He'd probably try to stop me from donating. Best to keep this from him for now. I'll tell him later—when it's time to move the silver dollars."

Everyone was happy and jumped onto the cloud, which soared into the sky and floated with the wind.

If you want to see how Monkey-King dazzles at an American school, tune in to the next chapter!

Figure 18 He caught sight of a few Americans seated in the pavilion's main hall, all in suits and ties, exuding a gentlemanly air. Adam was speaking with two or three of them.

Chapter 17: Pigsy Digging a Pit to Bury Silver and Facing Public Wrath

Pigsy Attempts to Outsmart the IRS by Burying Silver

Pigsy, carrying his iron rake, stepped into the courtyard and began furiously digging beneath a large oak tree. As he worked, he muttered, "You blind IRS, coming after me for taxes? I'll bury the silver in this pit and see how you manage to find it!"

But the oak tree was a centuries-old giant, with thick, tangled roots that constantly snagged his rake. Frustrated beyond reason, Pigsy started striking the tree in anger. The trunk shook, and a barrage of acorns rained down, covering him in dirt. He shouted in pain and frustration, while birds hurriedly flew away from the branches, sensing disaster coming.

Covered in dirt, Pigsy shook himself and shouted, "You old tree dared to hurt me? Today I'll knock you down!"

He lifted his rake again, pounding the tree even harder without stopping.

Locals Protest — Pigsy Reverts to His Original Form to Show His Strength

Hearing the commotion, several students from the martial arts school rushed outside and tried to stop him. "This tree is a protected landmark of New York, Class I status!" they cried. "You can't touch it like that, wild!"

But Pigsy wasn't about to back down; that was losing face in public.

He thought to himself, "These Americans have been looking down on me lately, thinking I'm no match for that Monkey-King. Why not show off a little, let the juniors see what I can do?"

With a few loud grunts, he tossed the rake aside, fell to the ground, and revealed his proper form — a towering, majestic black boar.

A poem celebrates his praise:

> Among the five beasts[31] tamed, the pig is the best,
> A farmer's true treasure, above all the rest.
> He eats, he naps, growing plump and wide,
> Praised by all people, both near and far beside.

The onlookers were stunned. Pigsy rammed the tree three times, causing the massive trunk to crash down. He jumped into the hole and dug ferociously, sending dirt flying in all directions. In no time, he had created a hill from the loose soil.

Climbing out of the pit, Pigsy announced, "This hole is seventy meters deep. Even if the IRS hears about it, there's no way they'll dig this far!"

He urged others to help throw the silver dollars into the pit.

But at that moment, a jet of clean water burst from the bottom of the pit and shot up into the sky. It turned out that Pigsy had unknowingly hit an underground water main or utility pipes, mistaking them for tree roots, and had broken them.

Neighbors Revolt — A Riot Breaks Out

Just as everyone stood stunned, a loud shout rang out. Hundreds of angry locals rushed out from nearby houses, armed with sticks and clubs, surrounding the martial arts school.

---

[31] Five tamed beasts generally refer to cow, horse, sheep, pig, dog in Chinese farm life.

A burly, shirtless man stepped forward and shouted at Pigsy, "You stupid immigrant! Digging holes and busting up water mains and power lines?! We, neighbors, have put up with your noisy martial arts school for too long. Today we've had enough! We're catching you today and taking you to the authorities! Surrender now! Hi, what are you waiting for?"

Before Pigsy could respond, five or six strong men rushed at him with ropes, trying to tie him up.

Pigsy erupted in fury and raised his iron rake, fighting fiercely. His American disciples from the martial arts school weren't about to give up either. This was a fierce fight. Hundreds of people, armed with clubs, surrounded him and the school from all directions.

A fierce battle broke out, spilling from the courtyard to the rooftops, from the martial arts school hall into the city streets. The chaos intensified so much that it seemed as if the heavens darkened, and even the sun and moon lost their light.

Why the Neighbors Were So Upset with the Martial Arts School

Dear readers, you might be curious about what exactly the martial arts school did to upset the entire neighborhood.

Well, ever since Pigsy opened this martial arts school and his Chinese friends moved in, the place has become a hub for visitors from China. Many tour groups or Chinese official delegations stay for two or three days at a time. These new immigrants also like to visit here first before moving to other cities. Every day, the kitchen buzzes with the sizzle and crackle of cooking. The thick smoke from cooking hangs in the air, intensified by America's abundant farms: fresh vegetables, fruits, meats, fish, poultry, eggs—all year round. These reasons attract the art school's guests to stay and cook.

Pigsy even hired two full-time cooks who followed cookbooks to create new dishes every day, never repeating a meal for him. The gluttonous Pigsy feasted eagerly, his mouth always greasy, as if he had been hungry for a thousand years. Every meal was a relief.

Pigsy was lazy by nature, and his crew of young greenhorns wasn't much better. They never cleaned their kitchen. The kitchen smelled strange, and everything was sticky. The floors were greasy, the window screens were covered in oil and grime, and cockroaches, mice, and bugs scurried everywhere.

What truly enraged the neighbors was garbage collection day. While other neighbors put out neat bags of bottles and cans, the martial arts school dumped out piles of fish bones, chicken heads, leftover stew, and spoiled soup. In hot weather, the stench attracted swarms of flies, mosquitoes, and rats. Even pigeons and other crews often fly over looking for food. Pedestrians avoided the sidewalk, and surrounding homes kept windows tightly shut.

Americans are known for their love of new products and their disdain for old ones. They replace household items quickly and throw away many used objects, from clothes and durable appliances to furniture—almost everything you can think of. Corporations are eager to market their products to consumers, and many are designed as throwaway items. The frugal Chinese immigrants walking the streets often felt it was a shame to let discarded things go to waste. They would pick them up and bring them home, where they would use or repair them. When these items accumulated, they could be a problem for a neighborhood. This goes without saying.

Pigsy and the others had long gotten used to this and never realized how much their neighbors scorned them. They simply carried on as usual—until today's explosive confrontation.

Pigsy Tries to Reason, but the Crowd Insists on His Move-Out

Spotting an opening, Pigsy leapt out of the circle and shouted, "Hold on! I've got something to say. I was digging a hole in my own yard—what business is that of yours? Why are you all ganging up and attacking me?"

The crowd responded, "First, you need approval from the city to do construction. No work without a permit!" But that's not the main issue. You've been choking the whole block with your cooking smoke day after day. And now today you're kicking up dust and noise, digging holes, and making a mess. How are we supposed to live? We won't rest until you're dealt with! We're telling you plainly—pack your things and get out!"

Pigsy Fights Back, But the Ninja Turtles Arrive on the Scene

Pigsy refused to back down. "You disrespectful idiot!" he shouted and started swinging his iron rake wildly at the crowd.

These were ordinary folks, untrained in martial arts and driven by sheer frustration. They were no match for Pigsy. In just a few rounds, they were huffing and puffing, gradually losing the fight.

Suddenly, a battle cry sounded—and four Ninja Turtles emerged from the water-filled pit, each wielding their own weapon: sword, fork, whip, and staff. They charged at Pigsy, and an intense new fight began.

Maybe because Pigsy was tired from digging, or perhaps because it was a surprise, Pigsy was caught off guard. He stumbled and fell to the ground. The turtles quickly tied him up with a rope.

Pigsy cried out, "Hey! Brave warriors—where are you from? I've got no beef with you. Why are you helping them fight me?"

One of the turtles responded, "We live in the city's sewer system—we're your underground neighbors, whether you realize it or not. And yet every day you dump leftover scraps and grease down the drain, clogging our paths and making our home smell worse. We've put up with this for too long. Enough is enough!"

Seeing the Ninja Turtles had restrained the troublemaker, the neighbors cheered. But they didn't seek revenge with fists or kicks—instead, they lifted Pigsy and carried him toward City Hall, demanding justice.

The procession was large and loud. Bystanders paused to watch, whispering and discussing among themselves, whether right or wrong. Yesterday, Pigsy was a hero in New York City; today, he is in doubt!

Pigsy Faces the Authorities

Inside City Hall, a police officer untied Pigsy. Looking up, Pigsy saw the commissioner sitting high on the platform, flipping through a folder. Behind him hung the flags of both the federal and state governments. Secretaries and aides stood respectfully nearby, while a line of officers along the wall held their arms behind their backs, glaring like wolves. Pigsy thought to himself, "A wise man yields to avoid trouble—let's see how this guy talks."

Moments later, the commissioner sat up straight and barked, "Pigsy! You rabble-rouser! Last time you wrecked that buffet shop—have you learned nothing? And now you dare stir up the whole neighborhood? By state law, toppling a protected tree, digging without a permit, and damaging public utilities are all serious crimes. What do you have to say for yourself?"

Pigsy replied, "Sir, I only dug the hole to bury some silver dollars I recently earned. My neighbors saw and got jealous, then gathered a mob to steal it!"

The commissioner raised his eyebrow and paused at the mention of silver. "Silver? That's good news. But why bury it? Is this money ill-gotten?"

Pigsy quickly explained, "The IRS is hunting me for taxes. I buried it so they wouldn't find it."

The secretaries and officers burst into laughter. The commissioner chuckled along, amused by Pigsy's honesty. Readers should understand that everyone tries to evade taxes, but no one has ever tried to hide it this way before.

"We've supported your martial arts in school," the commissioner said, "and offered jobs to your community. But now you're dodging taxes and shaming me in the process. By right stipulation, I should shut down your place. But considering you're a minority with limited means, I'll show leniency this time.

"Pay the taxes in full, fill in the hole, replant the tree, and restore the landscaping. Also, pay a fine of 500 silver taels to repair the utility lines. You have a lot of silver now, right?"

But the neighbors weren't satisfied. A representative stepped forward, "Pigsy is the blight of our neighborhood! This used to be a peaceful, quiet area. Since the martial arts school opened, people have come in droves—tens, even hundreds at a time—clogging the streets with parked cars and noise.

"The school is constantly filled with frying and cooking, choking us with smoke. Pigsy and his crew aren't poor—they're just cheap. They won't even bag their garbage! Flies, mosquitoes, stray dogs, rats—our property values have plummeted. We won't rest until he's evicted!"

Pigsy roared in protest: "Why are you all so eager to find faults with me? Think about how good I am! Since my martial arts school opened, business on this street has exploded! You set up stalls and make easy money, yet instead of working hard yourselves, you blame me! Do you even know how many tourism zones are begging me to open schools in New York City boroughs and across the country?"

One aide whispered to the commissioner, "These Chinese don't speak the language well. A harsh notice would scare them off. Scold them hard—they'll back down."

But the commissioner shook his head, "This matter can't be handled like the usual. Pigsy has a senior brother, Monkey-King, a warrior so fierce that not even celestial troops can catch him. If we anger him, we'll be the ones in trouble. Besides, the martial school did bring in tourism and money."

Another aide chimed in, "Then maybe separate Pigsy and Monkey-King first, then use high economic pressure."

The commissioner smiled, "You all only see their flaws, not their strengths. But I have a plan to turn trouble into opportunity."

He turned to Pigsy and said, "Mr. Pigsy, don't go running off to other development zones just yet. The root of the neighborhood's anger is falling property values. If you can raise them, everything will be fine.

"Land Spirits, those who oversee real estate, manage Feng Shui. If you could work with them to do something to suppress bad energy, drive away drug dealers, reduce crime, keep pests and diseases at bay, ward off evil, and promote harmony, this entire area could thrive. I believe the neighbors would be happy to support you.

I hear that your brother, Monkey-King, is respected by land spirits across the land. And you—you're the grandmaster of the iron rake, famous citywide. Can you tame the local evils and turn this around? If not, maybe your brother can help?

Pigsy's Tall Tales Flip the Script – Gold Trees Ignite a Real Estate Boom

Dear readers, although Pigsy is usually easygoing and kind, he absolutely hates it when others try to pressure him by bringing up Monkey-King. Hearing the commissioner's suggestion involving Monkey-King, Pigsy instantly flared up.

He claimed, "Sure, I can do it and handle everything in the best way. You only know land spirits fear Monkey's iron staff—but that doesn't mean they listen to him! They're actually pals with me. Back in the day, when I farmed in Gao Village, those land gods practically worshiped me. Whatever I planted, it thrived—melons produced melons, beans produced beans. I even planted an acre of gold trees, and at harvest time, not a single silver coin appeared. All gold! I brought my father-in-law a big farm and a big house—that was a major prestige—it was a blast!"

The commissioner's eyebrow arched, and his eyes lit up immediately as he said, "Melons and beans growing from seeds is biology—no surprise. But gold trees? Sounds like a tall tale. Gold doesn't grow on trees!"

Pigsy froze for a second—this commissioner was sharper than he thought. But he stood by his story, "I planted gold, and a gold tree grew. It gave chunk after chunk of gold. When it hit the ground, it nearly knocked me out; the gold lay everywhere, shining everywhere. How could that be fake?"

The commissioner lit up with delight, "If you can grow gold trees around your martial arts school, and of course, enable the parcels in the area to grow too, the neighbors will get rich—they'll be thrilled!"

Pigsy panicked a little in his mind—Gold trees aren't exactly easy to grow!—but kept bluffing, "Planting a grove is no big deal... I worry the local soil might not take, and the trees won't bear full chunks of gold."

Hearing this, the angry neighbors immediately set aside their grudges over the grease, trash, and noise. They knelt, pleading, "Immortal sir, just do your best! Even if the trees don't produce full-sized good bricks—gold beans, gold flakes—anything is fine too, great news!"

The commissioner, now elated beyond belief, said, "Mr. Pigsy, with this kind of power, your fame will outshine even that monkey's!"

He then continued after a pause, "You see, I have a vacant house on a quiet street. To solve the smoke problem for the people, I'm willing to rent it to you at a very low cost, just for your living and cooking. I know you've been trying to bring your wife here to enjoy life. She's finally arrived—you shouldn't make her suffer to save a few bucks. It's unworthy of your title as Eastern Saint Monk and Holy Altar Marshal. Don't worry about rent—I'll waive it entirely. Just grow me a few gold trees in the backyard when you have time."

Pigsy replied, "I heard buying or renting property helps reduce taxes. Since the commissioner himself is offering, I'll go home and talk it over with my wife."

Everyone quickly gathered around and escorted Pigsy back to the martial arts school, laughing and chatting the whole way— dreaming of forests full of gold trees. Onlookers stared in confusion: How had the neighborhood conflict suddenly turned into a joyful parade?

That very day, property prices in the martial arts district skyrocketed. The sale of houses suddenly halted—not because of low market demand, but because nobody wanted to sell. New York real estate listings added a whole new category beside "ocean-view" and "school district": "Golden Tree Hamlet."

But that's a tale for another day.

After the crowd dispersed, the commissioner laughed joyfully, "What a smart idea! I've kept the peace, made the people happy, and earned their praise. None of your clever tactics could match this." The secretaries and aides all nodded eagerly, showering the commissioner with compliments for his vision and foresight.

To know what happens next—stay tuned for the next chapter.

Figure 19 Pigsy looked up and saw the commissioner seated high on the dais, flipping through a thin booklet. Behind him, the wall displayed the flags of the federal and state governments, while several secretaries and attendants bowed respectfully. Along the wall stood a row of police officers, hands folded, each looking fierce as a wolf or tiger. Pigsy thought to himself, "A hero does not try if not sure of success."

Chapter 18: Monkey-King Scouts Talent in Rhode Island — Somersault Lessons Inspire Youngsters

A Picturesque Island Away from the City Crowds

Along the Atlantic shores, scattered like stars across the sea, lie a few islands. Among them is one of unmatched charm: Rhode Island. Mountains cradle it, waters embrace it, forests flourish with lush greenery, rocks form curious shapes, and meadows bloom like brocade. Seagulls glide in the sky, and pigeons flash their wings above white houses nestled among green trees. A church spire pierces the clouds, and the bell tolls with a peaceful sound that carries for miles.

The island reflects the architectural imprint of its immigrant founders—elegant and diverse homes arranged like constellations. The air has an old-world charm. The islanders, men and women alike, dress neatly and carry themselves with poised grace. Generations have been raised under European tradition, and they proudly call themselves "Rhode Islanders"—a name meant to distinguish them from cities. Though just 200 miles (about four hours' drive) from the well-known yet notorious City of New York, they see themselves as a world apart, both in spirit and culture.

On this peaceful island, there's a private school set between the mountains and the sea. Positioned in privacy, it serves only the children of the elite, teaching them with great attention to detail.

You, my dear reader, might ask, "Isn't America a land of equality? Why such exclusivity?" A fair question. In reality, the law prevents any school from openly declaring itself as exclusive to aristocrats only. Therefore, the school's admission banner reads nobly, "All are welcome, regardless of status, race, or background. Equal opportunity for all."

But a closer look reveals tuition fees exceeding 90,000 silver taels a year—enough to make common folk blanch. Truly, only wealthy and prestigious families can afford to enter. Occasionally, talented individuals from lower classes may be chosen to join, further enhancing the school's prestige.

Monkey-King Visits as a Donor

News of Monkey-King's recent pledge to support education and donate funds spread quickly. The Rhode Island academy, learning of his fame, promptly invited him to visit.

On a beautiful spring day—cool breezes and blooming flowers—Monkey-King arrived on campus, accompanied by trustees and administrators. He observed stately buildings rising among the trees, with red walls and green copper roofs peeking through the greenery. Boys in long pants and girls in skirts moved with graceful ease. Everyone was clean, well-mannered, and had bright eyes, all in a joyful mood.

Monkey-King smiled broadly. He said, "I've long heard of America's wealth and scientific progress. I've wanted to see how you educate your youth. Although I've traveled widely across many lands, I've yet to visit a true center of learning. Today, given this opportunity, I ask you to show me your best methods—so that my donation will be meaningful."

The headmaster bowed and replied, "Our school has thrived for over a century. Many of our students go on to Ivy League schools and then spread across the world. Quite a few have earned renown and a place in history. Great Sage, I promise this visit will not disappoint you."

But Monkey-King frowned upon hearing this. "Ivy schools?" he scoffed. "To me, they don't offer much. Though full of strange theories and clever tricks, they lack a true understanding of Heaven and Earth. You dwell far from the East and only know the limited teachings of the West. I love seeing you students. If I find a worthy student, I will guide them toward Chinese philosophy. Do not mislead the young with shallow doctrines!"

The headmaster, surprised, forced a smile and bowed again. "The land of the East, home of tea, silk, and calligraphy, holds many wonders," he said. "I often talk about them to my students, too." But secretly, this is what the schoolmaster muttered, "So the stories are true—Chinese really do love to boast. We Westerners flatter them openly but rarely mean it. This monkey is no exception. If it weren't for his silver dollars, who would bother to be around him?"

A Diplomatic Proposal: East Meets West

A trustee, fearing Monkey-King might take the donation and leave, quickly offered a solution, "Please, Great Sage, do not be upset. We have a school policy that donors may direct where their funds go. If your wish is to promote Eastern learning, why not create an Eastern Studies Fund? We could build a special institute within our school—an Eastern Academy. Fill it with classic Chinese texts, invite scholars to lecture, and let students absorb the wisdom of your homeland. And if a few gifted students receive personal instruction from you, their future success would reflect both your teaching and our shared purpose. Would this not serve all sides?"

Monkey-King's expression softened. "Your words are pleasing, but the path is hard. Since my travels to India to obtain the scriptures, my fame has spread worldwide. Many seek to study with me, but I am strict in choosing disciples. All must have moral strength, sharp minds, and physical vitality—I will not accept anyone who falls short. Even after traveling the world, I have yet to find someone worthy. I now teach only my monkeys on Flower-Fruit Mountain, and spend my time writing and studying the past and present."

The trustees and administrators all bowed. The trustee board chairman insisted, "Our students come from the finest families. They are raised with discipline and education from birth. In virtue, intellect, and strength, they surely meet your standards. Here, let me show you the beautiful campus and talented students."

After a short walk, Monkey-King said, "Yes, a gorgeous campus. Are you people only showing off the grandest halls and hiding the dirt in the corners? But I prefer the hidden places. Take me through the quiet paths and shadowed alleys. That is where I'll find the truth."

With no choice, they led him along a coastal trail. Trees arched overhead, waves crashed nearby, grasses grew wild, and seabirds called above. Monkey-King looked around, his heart swelling with joy.

Lifting his face toward the sky, he exclaimed, "What a marvel this world is! Such harmony of Heaven and Earth—surely not made by human hands!"

A Promising Student by the Shore

As they lingered, a sudden voice reading aloud from a book rang out clearly in the sea breeze. The group turned to see, at some distance on a bench by the shore, a youth seated with a book resting on his knee, reading aloud with a voice full of clarity, oblivious to everything around him.

The headmaster's face lit up with joy as he turned to Monkey-King, "The boy is fifteen — the pride of our school! He is a third-generation descendant of the Morgan family. Not only does he possess a mind capable of charting the star constellations in the sky and governing nations on earth, but he also has a heart to uplift the world's weary and distressed. He studies both ethics and management science, and often compares himself to Bill Gates. Truly a pillar of America's new century! Would the Immortal accept him as a disciple?"

Monkey-King nodded and said, "He appears diligent and well-mannered. He reads with earnestness. Perhaps he is a youth of character. Let me test his integrity."

With that, Monkey-King approached the boy and said, "Fortune favors you, young man; you enjoy studying on your own."

The boy looked puzzled. Monkey-King asked, "I wish to ask you a question to test your judgment — may I?"

The youth stood up and replied respectfully, "Yes, sir."

Monkey-King asked, "If I, your elder and teacher, wished to lie on this bench for a short nap, would you give up your seat and leave?"

The youth met Monkey-King's gaze with steady eyes and a proud stance and said, "For what reason should I yield to you? Please explain."

Monkey-King replied, "Society is organized by rank. So are schools. Elders and teachers are at the top, and students are at the bottom. Those higher in status claim the seat; those lower must give way."

The boy answered, "I can give up my seat for the sick, but not for your reason. Pardon my honesty, your logic is flawed. If a teacher is tired or unwell, I would of course yield — that is kindness. If a visitor comes to enjoy the view, I'd do the same — that is courtesy. If a child comes to play, I'd also yield — that is compassion. But social rank alone should not determine who stays or goes. Let it be decided by who arrives first. The first to arrive has the right; later ones must move on. Rank exists in society, yes — but in competition, it carries no weight. Competition is based only on fairness."

Monkey-King could not help but laugh. When the trustees and headmaster caught up, he recounted the conversation and added, "In China, we prize virtue from the cradle. Even at three, a child learns to offer the better pear to elders. Why, then, do your youths speak only of timing, fairness, and not of deference in age and social rankings? How shall someone with such conduct navigate human relations and win hearts from those above and below? If each person insists on their own rights, how can the masses build prosperity together? At best, he becomes just another rich man. I take disciples who do not do so for private gain but to serve those who suffer before seeking joy for themselves. How can this youth match that calling?"

The headmaster smiled and replied, "Then may I speak plainly? America is a society of competition. Without that drive, how can anyone stand out? Did not Your Excellency once storm the heavens and shout, 'The throne rotates—next year it shall be mine!'[32] You yourself defied your own rank as a monkey in the wild—how can you now fault this boy?"

---

[32] This was a quote of what MonkeyKing said in his rebellious revolt in Heaven fight.

Monkey-King laughed and then said, "Well said! You turn my words around on me. A taste of my own medicine! I admire his courage. He fears neither heaven nor earth. May he not lose this spirit to the hardships of life. Alas, our Chinese children follow rules too closely and worship authority blindly. Different nations, different teachings."

Monkey-King's Flipping Fitness Plan

They moved on to the athletic field, where boys and girls leaped and played energetically — lively, cheerful, and full of energy.

A trustee said, "Though secluded in Rhode Island, we have long heard of the Great Sage's mighty power — vanquishing demons, subduing spirits, and renowned for martial skill. Would you teach our students a few tricks?"

Monkey-King clapped his hands happily, "Your words touch my heart! Cloud-travel and the seventy-two transformations require a divine root — not easily taught. But perhaps I can select a few bright children and teach them how to somersault. When they learn it, though they may not fly a thousand miles in an instant — at least they'll be able to run fast, and better than crawling around in those clunky iron wagons!"

The headmaster beamed. "The Great Sage has truly fiery eyes that pierce through illusion. Our American children, overfed and sedentary, suffer from overweight bodies. If your somersaulting can shape them into forms like yours — even without the cloud-riding — we shall be most fortunate and grateful!"

Readers unfamiliar with America might not understand why the board was so excited. The truth is, many international visitors are shocked by the size of Americans. The claim that America leads the world in body weight is certainly not an exaggeration.

Living on junk food, rarely walking, never riding in cars and elevators, indulging in sweets while watching television—how can such habits not lead to overweight bodies? Childhood obesity is a problem in schools. Seven or eight out of ten children are overweight. Then, in adulthood, there are waves of disease—heart failure, diabetes—that drive up healthcare costs and worry the nation. One expert once warned, "At this rate, should a world war erupt, America would have no soldiers fit to fight!"

Regulations and Resistance

Monkey-King, fond of praise, got excited and rolled up his sleeves. "Bring the children—I'll begin training!"

But the board frantically waved its hands. "Please wait! Though well-intentioned, any new activity must be approved by parents first. Consent forms need to be signed. If even one child sprains an ankle, we would be liable. Slow and careful is best."

Monkey-King frowned. "Learning my skills requires bumps and bruises! In our custom, once a student is handed over to a master, life or death is not questioned. I've given you silver—must I also beg the parents? Call the students! Enough chatter! I know how to ensure safety."

The headmaster, trembling yet tempted by the donation, called for the children—over a hundred lined up eagerly.

Upon hearing they'd learn somersaults, the children cheered and jumped with joy. They followed Monkey-King to the lawn and started to roll. But consider this: American children, well-fed since birth and nourished on milk and candy, are often strong in build but also carry extra weight. Flipping is a full-body exercise, and very few could do it well. They managed to do cartwheels and somersaults quite well. However, after three or five flips, they were breathless, sweating heavily, and hiding under trees with cold drinks in hand.

Monkey-King was furious. "Continue!" he barked.

The headmaster pleaded, "Please, Great Sage, don't push them too hard. Here, education is based on freedom. Teachers cannot force unwilling students."

Monkey-King's Ground Golden Ring

Monkey-King grew angrier and said, "What are these absurd rules? Without discipline, how can they be forged?" He pulled his golden stick from his ear and twirled it in the grass.

Alarmed, the headmaster thought, "We're finished! That stick will leave them dead or injured!"

But Monkey-King simply drew a large gold circle on the ground and blew a puff of spirit breath. Within seconds, dozens of children inside the circle flipped head-over-heels as if wound up by gears—some laughing like on a swing, some screaming as if on a roller coaster. But they all cannot stop.

The board and faculty, despite their experience in school matters, had never encountered such a method. Their jaws dropped. They moaned in confusion, powerless to act.

After a while, Monkey-King waved his hand again. The children eased their jumps and landed safely, panting heavily. Faculty rushed forward, only to see the children light on their feet, full of energy; their obesity had disappeared.

Praise for the Monkey's Miracle

The headmaster exclaimed with joy, "Your powers are truly boundless. We are in awe!"

Another director added, "Obesity has plagued us for far too long. We spent fortunes with little effect. The Great Sage has solved it in a day!"

They sectioned off the golden circle to prevent it from being trampled and erased.

Monkey-King chuckled, "In the East, we teach with both pressure and patience. Bitter hardship breeds excellence.' Here, you indulge freely, and the results are poor. Take this method and make it your own. Each day, have the children flip within the circle. They'll slim down and grow strong—like me. I've given you silver—now I give you this ground golden ring.

The headmaster bowed repeatedly, "Such wisdom, profound and admirable."

The Circle Expands, the Obsession Starts

Though Monkey-King's methods seemed harsh, the results were clear. Staff and students alike gathered around the circle, eager to give it a try. Even the janitors, porters, and gardeners took turns. For so long, they had lived uncomfortably, growing fat without working. Now they hoped a few flips could help shed some of that fat.

The golden ring expanded on its own, accommodating everyone who stepped in. And everyone who entered kept flipping— until their weight matched the standard.

A Poem in Its Praise

One cherishes freedom.
One bears the chosen weight.
One dances through the spring;
One works from dawn till late.

One plants trees for cooling shade,
One trains steeds swift-hooved for the race.
One raises gentle hands in patience, soft and shy;
One rules with a harsh voice and unwavering eye.

And in the end—
One catches the moon's reflection from the water in the pond,
The other plucks flowers from the silent mirror so fond.

—But that's a story for another time.

Figure 20 Monkey-King, being one who delighted in praise, could not help himself after the academy supervisor's exhortations. He promptly tightened his belt, rolled up his sleeves, and urged the supervisor to gather the children in line for practice. Unexpectedly, the board members waved their hands frantically, repeatedly exclaiming, "Not allowed!"

Chapter 19: Planting Flowers to Rescuing the Butterfly; Defeating the Demon Fish in Watersports

It is said that the United States of America is a land of high capitalism, where individualism is revered, and wealth is pursued above all else. This is true to an extent. However, to believe that the nation only worships individualism, ignoring public interests and the common good, would be incorrect. Why is that? Let's consider the example of the national parks.

The vast American land, once an untamed wilderness with majestic mountains, pristine lakes, and unique geological wonders, mainly remained untouched until the 1800s. Around that time, a few cowboys began advocating for preserving nature in its pure form. They proposed creating national parks, not for profit, so that future generations could enjoy the beauty of unspoiled lands. You might say, "What's so surprising about setting aside some uninhabited land for public use?" But this would be a hasty judgment. The challenge of the world lies in being the first to do this. The idea of a national park was an unprecedented decision in human history. Once a model is established, it becomes easier for others to follow.

These pioneers not only built the parks but also established the principles of preservation: they remain forever wild. What they started has largely continued unchanged to this day. Still, the core of national parks rests on two key ideals: first, preventing commercial exploitation to protect wilderness; second, ensuring public access—always with preservation in mind. Today, hundreds of national parks stretch across the country from east to west. Acadia, on the Atlantic coast in Maine, is just one example. This is where our story will continue.

One day, Monkey-King, with not much to do, heard of Acadia's beauty. He jumped onto a white cloud and drifted toward Maine. From above, he saw crashing waves, steep peaks, lush greenery, and abundant waters. As he descended slowly, he prepared to enjoy the scenery—when suddenly, a vibrant swarm of butterflies whirled past, obscuring even the sun. Thousands? No, millions! Monkey-King hurried to land and gazed upward. In the sky, countless butterflies fluttered and danced, chasing each other joyfully. Then, as if petals blown by the wind, they descended into flowered meadows—an ethereal sight, unmatched in splendor.

Dear reader, this was the famous monarch butterfly migration of the Americas—a journey from the north to the south, crossing mountain ranges, lakes, and plains, from Canada through the United States, all the way to Mexico. Among the hundreds of butterfly species, only the monarch embarks on this epic flight—a marvel of nature, repeated for millions of years on delicate wings, carried by winds both strange and familiar.

Monkey-King, always playful, transformed into a butterfly and joined the swirling dance, drifting with the breeze. After an hour of flying, he grew tired, settled among the flowers, looked at the clouds, and listened to the murmuring streams in the meadows. Gradually, he drifted into a dream.

A poem says:

> In a butterfly dream, he wandered far,
> On wings of wind, where wonders are.
> The tale of migration, ancient and deep,
> Through sky and bloom, in dream and sleep.

The Monarch Butterfly's Plight

Then suddenly, Monkey-King heard voices nearby:

"Hey, this butterfly is too strange—so much larger than the others! And it has a long tail!"

"A genetic mutation, surely!"

"And look—its colors are unusual. Shall we tag it for study?"

"Great Sage! Wake up! Wake up!" another voice shouted from behind.

Startled, Monkey-King leapt up—but to his dismay, his arms were restrained. He looked around — he had been captured.

"Let me go!" he cried.

It turned out that a group of girl students was conducting a butterfly count. One of them had caught Monkey-King.

"Who are you? Why are you disguised as a butterfly?"

Monkey-King hesitated and thought to himself, "For the Great Sage Equal to Heaven to be caught by a girl—what shame! Better to fool her and escape."

So he said, "I am a Butterfly Immortal. If you release me into the sky, I shall grant you one wish."

The girl replied, "I will, but let me tag you first." She attached a label to Monkey-King's wing, then tossed him into the air. Monkey-King immediately reverted to his usual form and landed nearby. The students were amazed.

"Who never knew a monarch butterfly could transform like that, monkey?" they exclaimed, crowding around to question him.

Monkey-King asked, "With millions of butterflies, how can you possibly count them? Why not stay in class instead of wasting effort here?"

"You must be from somewhere else, sir, and perhaps don't know," said one student, "that these butterflies have declined sharply in recent years. We have been collecting and analyzing data annually in hopes of understanding how quickly they are disappearing."

Monkey-King, noticing the students' anxious faces, felt compassion swell in his heart. He asked, "And what is the cause of their decline?"

A young girl replied, "The land has endured repeated pollution. The milkweed that monarch butterflies rely on can no longer grow. Recently, we've encouraged every household to plant milkweed in their gardens. The response has been warm, but it's like a cup of water on a burning cart — of little help. You previously granted me a wish — may I now ask you to restore the meadows and scatter milkweed seeds along the butterflies' migration path?"

Monkey-King replied, "A sharp drop in the monarch population is surely no good omen. It worries me as well." Then, pointing upward, he said, "Look to the sky — who comes there?" With that, he began to recite an incantation.

The crowd looked skyward. In the clear blue above, approaching from a distance, a host of celestial maidens dressed in flowing garments of rainbow colors appeared. Each carried a bamboo basket and had a hoe slung over her shoulder.

Monkey-King soared into the air to meet them. "You, who are skilled in planting flowers and grass, why not help these students with a noble deed? Go now, and sow milkweed across the world."

The fairies rejoiced at his words. Laughing and cheerful with the schoolgirls, they together select good land and cast large handfuls of milkweed seed into the breeze. As the seeds fell to the ground, a gentle rain began to fall, soft and misty. In a moment, the seeds sprouted and grew — flowers swayed in the wind in red, yellow, blue, and green. Butterflies fluttered happily among them, and the earth bloomed with life and color.

A poem in praise:

> When monarchs ride the cooling air,
> They cross vast lands, unbowed, aware.
> Their wings may seem soft and light—
> Yet home they head to in arduous flight.

Trouble on the Great Lakes

Let us not dwell further on how monarchs migrated smoothly that year, with milkweed flourishing in their path home, and how the butterflies enjoyed a remarkable population comeback. Instead, let us return to Monkey-King, who, having done a good deed, made his way back toward New York now.

Passing over the Great Lakes, he looked down to see a vast expanse of water — the waves rising with the wind, the horizon barely visible in mist, sailboats dotting the lake like scattered leaves. Monkey-King sighed, "In olden days, the Mongols called lakes 'seas' [33]— and rightly so!"

Just then, a man on one of the boats fell into the water. Speedboats started racing across the surface, searching quickly.

---

[33] In many parts of Northern China today, it is common to find places named 'sea' believed to be big lakes in history.

Monkey-King, confused by what he saw, was about to investigate when suddenly Pigsy burst from beneath the water, crying, "Monkey Brother, help me!"

A group of patrol boats chased and surrounded him. They were part of the Federal Environmental Protection Agency's Water Patrol Division.

Recognizing Monkey-King as a senior New York government official, the officers respectfully explained the situation, issued a citation, and released Pigsy.

But what had happened?

It turns out that Pigsy, a devout Buddhist, had made a vow to release captive creatures as an offering of thanks after his arm healed and his rake was recovered. This was a common practice in Buddhist tradition, as Pigsy always believed. On an auspicious, favorable day, he took several carp, each two feet long, and released them into the lake — only to be caught in the act by environmental patrol officers.

Unwilling to argue with lawmen and confident in his past as Marshal Tianpeng, master of the waters, Pigsy yelled, "Away I go!" and dove deep into the lake. But the patrol boats were quick and persistent, weaving and circling until Monkey-King arrived just in time to save him.

A Citation Ignored, Trouble Brews

Now, dear reader, a citation isn't a big deal — just a hundred dollars or so, easily paid by mail. But Pigsy stubbornly insisted, "Releasing life is a meritorious Buddhist act — not a crime!" Confident in his martial skills, he mocked the citation, tore it up, and threw it in the trash.

"If they dare come collect," he muttered, "I'll knock them over and put a few holes in them!"

Monkey-King, a high-ranking official with a steed and title in New York State, naturally faced no consequences. The inspectors, too, will let the matter slide. Monkey-King and Pigsy both forgot this citation and never imagined it would come back to haunt them.

And so, reader, understand this: immigrants from foreign lands often have a weak sense of legal obligation. Although they live in America, their old habits linger. A fine? Delay it as long as possible. The courts, reluctant to pursue minor infractions, rarely intervene unless more serious offenses occur. If Pigsy had stayed out of trouble, the case probably would have dissolved over time. However, this is not the case with Pigsy this time.

The Asian Carp Destroyed a Nation

A few months went by. One day, Monkey-King was checking the horse stables when an urgent message came in, "Pigsy is in trouble — come quickly to Lake Erie!"

What has happened now?

It turns out the carp Pigsy released were no ordinary fish — they were demonic creatures, condemned by Heaven and smuggled illegally into New York. Had they been cooked and eaten, no harm would have come. But once freed into the wild, they bred rapidly, multiplying by the tens of millions.

The native American fish, used to clean waters and gentle ecosystems, had never seen such foreign monsters. They were chased and eaten wherever they swam by the carp. In just a few months, the rivers and lakes of America fell into ecological chaos.

The demonic carp, with no natural predators, ruled supreme without any challenges.

Television stations broadcast the disaster live from the affected lakes, calling it the "Asian Demon Carp Crisis." The nation was shaken. The Department of Environment declared a state of emergency. Federal courts issued a warrant: Pigsy was to be apprehended immediately and brought to the scene of his crime, Lake Erie.

A Nation Rises, A Game Is Born

Monkey-King arrived to find the inspectors gnashing their teeth, furious enough to eat Pigsy alive. Adam and others were gathered, frantically seeking a solution. When they saw Monkey-King, they showed their respect.

"What's done is done," Monkey-King said. "Strict punishment is no remedy. What plan might rid us of these demon fish?"

"The government has installed underwater fences across the rivers to prevent the fish from spreading further," an officer replied.

"Great Sage," another asked, "your powers are vast. Might you devise a way to capture them all?"

I could use the water-empty spell to lift the lake's waters into the sky temporarily, then refill it after a storm — the demon fish would perish.

But another officer objected, "The fish would die, yes, but so would the insects, plants, and snails. The whole ecosystem would be destroyed. We cannot afford such a loss!"

Pigsy, embarrassed, stayed silent. Seeing that Monkey-King had no quick plan, he suggested, "Demon fish? Bah! They're just fat carp. Let the restaurants catch them. Let everyone feast! In no time, they'll be gone. Folks will grow fat and happy!"

Adam interjected, "That won't work. Carp have too many bones, and Westerners aren't used to them. Cowboys and cooks here only know grill and barbecue. We need a new idea."

Monkey-King scratched his head. "Could we not put chemicals in the lake?"

"Again," the officer warned, "that would kill everything — even the harmless. It's not an option."

Monkey-King sighed. "This is troublesome. To catch these many carp, in Eastern land, we usually find a way to mobilize the masses. We need to wage a 'people's campaign'. We must get as many people as possible to participate. Or else, I need to seek reinforcements elsewhere."

"Fear not, Great Sage," Adam said with a smile. "Look at that."

He pointed across the lake. There, two or three speed boats darted across the water. Wherever they passed, large carp leapt three to five feet into the air, in flashes of silver arc, before splashing back down again. Men and women on board jabbed with spears or scooped them up with nets in a contest of skill.

Adam said, "These demon fish, though bold underwater, have one quirk — when startled, they leap into the air. Americans love outdoor sports, especially water-based ones."

Monkey-King suddenly got excited and said to Adam, "Why not invent a new game competition: *Aerial Fishing*? Create rules, divide by gender and age, install sonar alarms on boats to startle the fish, then offer prizes for the most caught. Cash, medals, glory — who wouldn't join? Give it a year or two, and the demon fish will be no more."

Adam clapped his hands joyfully. "Wonderful! People's sports! We can offer tax incentives to those who participate, too."

Monkey-King raised his thumb, "You Ivy League students finally have good ideas this time around! You combine people's economic benefits, guiding them without force or tricks. This, I could not have thought of!"

So, the decision was made.

The Sport That Saved the Lakes

Now with no time to waste, Monkey-King and Pigsy began installing underwater alarms on any yachts and sailboats that volunteered, free of charge. They started boat-rental services at major lakes. Adam drafted a comprehensive rulebook for the Aerial Fishing competition, offered generous prizes for winners, and even set up participation gifts for every contestant — instantly redeemable.

Americans, always eager for thrills and new experiences, couldn't resist. Soon, they poured out of the cities and onto the lakes and rivers. Across the water, it was truly a sight to see:

A thousand sails racing,
A hundred boats circling,
Silver fish jumping, voices laughing.
And alas, the demon fish met their doom,

Driven out of their new home, they escape in vain.

But what happened to the brothers of Pigsy and Monkey-King? That, dear reader, will be revealed in the next chapter.

Figure 21 He slowly lowered his moving cloud, just about to appreciate the beautiful land, when, whoosh, he was hit by multicolored butterflies that swirled around him in a dazzling storm. They blotted out the sky and sun; not merely thousands of them, but truly hundreds of thousands—indeed, saying even millions would not be an exaggeration.

Chapter 20: Cultural Clash on the Charles River; Monkey-King Heads Eastern Plaza

Across the Continent, Monkey-King and Pigsy Capture Hearts

Many recent events have occurred in North America. Here are just a few. Pigsy defeated demons, and Monkey-King tamed fires—these heroic acts truly inspired genuine admiration among the people. In the Americas, where telecommunications stretched coast to coast, news of their legends quickly spread everywhere. Embellishments soon appeared. Word of mouth turned into more exaggerated tales: stories of Monkey-King slicing rainbows with his blade, or co-founding an insurance company with King Yama; of Pigsy swinging his nine-toothed rake against Black-wind devils; or how Buffett's business in New York suddenly skyrocketed.

In the blink of an eye, the Eastern Sage Monk Monkey-King became a household name. People mentioned his name on street corners; newspapers and magazines prominently featured him on their front pages with lavish details to feed hungry and eager readers. Colleges, whether modest or prestigious, rushed to host cultural lectures, inviting scholars and experts to analyze the differences between Eastern and Western cultures. For a time, no serious discussion could happen without mentioning Monkey-King—any scholar who failed to do so, no matter how knowledgeable, was politely ignored.

Pigsy also found no peace. His natural simplicity, quick wit, and clumsy honesty endeared him to the masses, earning him the title of top entertainment celebrity. Film studios competed for his likeness, and offers from the entertainment industry flooded in like spring rain. As the saying goes, when it rains, it pours.

Word Reaches Master Restivo: The Grand Master Notices

Loyal followers of Ivy League Schools quickly passed this news to the Grand Master of Ivy League, Master Restivo. The showdown is approaching.

My readers should understand this: America is a land where people from all nations come together. Faiths are many and free to be practiced; different sects and doctrines exist. To promote harmony, the government enforces a clear separation between church and state. Churches and spiritual groups handle moral and spiritual matters—teaching about good and evil—while steering clear of meddling in political issues.

Yet Master Restivo, though celebrated as a Grand Master in his time, paid little mind to formal religion. He had once studied Buddhism himself, but being naturally upright and fiercely independent, he often debated with his opponents beneath the lotus throne. Eventually, he declared, "Our ways and world are apart; we shall not be together," and embarked on a long journey—crossing oceans and wandering the world.

He eventually settled on the Western Continent, dedicating himself to grand strategies that promoted science and technology. He envisioned healing the world and leading nations. Among his followers were a few loyal disciples, each a rare talent, skilled not only in martial arts but also in governance. Guided by their advice, the United States rose to global dominance. Its political institutions, financial systems, legal frameworks, military strength, educational institutions, scientific advancements, industries, agriculture, environmental efforts, and athletic achievements all set global standards. Among the four great continents and hundreds of nations, none could rival its stature. It stood as the sole global superpower.

A Discourse on Charles River

On this day, Master Restivo stood by the Charles River in Boston, teaching several dozen disciples. Hearing the news of Monkey-King's arrival, he chuckled and said, "That monkey—I know him well. Years ago, he caused chaos in Heaven and was pressed beneath the Five Elements Mountain by the Supreme Buddha, Tathāgata. While most condemned him as deserving his fate, I alone felt compassion and showed him sympathy."

"Later, he defeated demons and helped the Tank monk retrieve scriptures from India, bringing enlightenment to the people of Tang who were in ignorance. However, his great deeds attracted the envy of Heaven itself. Jealous gods forced him back to his Flower-Fruit Mountain, where he isolated himself to study. Now, the Eastern Divine Continent is consumed by material desires, and people's hearts are restless—perhaps he has not yet found a quiet place to read. That's all I guessed."

At this, disciple Adam stepped forward and said, "Master, I recently encountered Monkey-King. His spiritual roots are deep and intense, his powers vast—surely, he is the true Sage Monk of the East. His brother Pigsy, though slothful and simple, possesses a kind heart and earns the affection of all people in America."

"I've long heard of your aim to bridge East and West, to enlighten deserving souls with culture and reason. Why not bring both into our world?

Master Restivo replied, "Monkey-King is titled 'Great Sage Equal to Heaven,' now known as 'Victorious Fighting Buddha'—

proud, unruly, and scornful of peers. Though I may wish it, he has no desire to submit.

"We must rely on the strength of American culture to handle him, to overcome him—not through force, but through influence and intimidation. That Monkey-King, blessed with spiritual essence and celestial origin, might someday grasp the mysteries of Western thought and rediscover the secrets of the East. When that day comes, we might even find ourselves outmatched. We aren't even going to be his worthy rivals."

The Roots of Civilization: Master Restivo Breaks Down the Human Journey

Adam bowed and said, "Master's vision for cultural exchange is profound. Though I follow you closely, I confess I still do not fully understand. Please elaborate."

Master Restivo said, "In the earliest ages, mankind was no different from wild beasts—gnawing raw flesh, drinking blood. Only half a million years ago, they were gifted with fire from the heavens—lightning in the sky—thereby discovering the miracle of cooked food."

"Still, they survived by gathering fruits in forests and hunting beasts on endless plains, wrapped in ignorance and darkness. Not until six thousand years ago did they learn to build villages, construct cities, and tame wild animals. At that time, not even a glimmer of civilization shone on the four continents.

"Two thousand years ago, cultural centers[34] Started to emerge. The East and West each followed their own paths,

---

[34] The civilization-axis theory was proposed by the German philosopher Karl Jaspers.

experiencing cycles of growth and decline. However, in recent decades, Western civilization, which thrived for two hundred years, has started to stagnate, gradually losing strength and slowly surrendering to the rising culture of the East.

Meanwhile, the Eastern Divine Continent thrives with vitality, governance remains steady, and society prospers. If Western civilization wants to slow down the Eastern rise, it must shed its arrogance and learn from the East, picking out what is good and adopting it. The beginning of this change starts with cultural exchange.

Taylor Objects: The Supremacy of Greece

At this moment, another disciple stepped forward—Dr. Taylor. He declared, "Master, your judgment is flawed! Greek civilization thundered across the world, awakening the deaf and blind! How can Confucius, Mencius, Laozi, or Zhuangzi compare?

"Today's science, technology, democracy, and law are all simply extensions of Greek thought. In developing modern sciences and technologies, the East has contributed nothing—not a single step forward! Eastern culture is merely fading away. Look at the once-glorious Mesopotamian 'Two Rivers' civilization—its towers once reached the sky. Where is it now? Forgotten, reduced to dust and ruins! I doubt China's current glory will last much longer."

Master Restivo Critiques Cultural Arrogance: Everything Must Pass

Master Restivo smiled and replied, "Such discourse is already outdated. 'All compounded things are impermanent; they are the law of birth and death.' All things under Heaven have their beginning and end—and within each beginning is an 'end of another'. There lies a web of hidden causes and conditions: emergence, flourishing, decline, and extinction.

"In the dawn of Heaven and Earth, many cultures rose in rivalry. Today, the civilizations of the Two Rivers and of the Maya have fallen silent and vanished. Only the Western Christian tradition and the Eastern Confucian legacy remain vigorous and alive. The others, though they struggle and resist, live like reeds in a storm—fighting to survive in narrow crevices, their fate bleak at best.

"You should read more broadly—books, newspapers, and global issues. Don't limit yourself to American media. Don't let yourself stay so uninformed."

Adam Questions the End: What Brings the Fall of Civilization?

Adam, moved by the words, stepped forward again and asked, "Master, your insight is unmatched. Just days ago, I studied the new Physics textbook and learned that no matter how impressive something may seem, no matter how much energy it has, it will eventually turn to dust, ash, and the Heat Death of the Universe— *Chaos takes place.*[35] The thought overwhelmed me, and I wept without knowing why.

"I was born in a later age, and I dare ask: by what cause does human culture perish? Where lies its downfall?"

Master Restivo answered solemnly, "The cosmic theory of 'Heat Death of the Universe' in your physics book is no new

---

[35] A cosmos theory.

doctrine. A thousand years ago, the Eastern scholar Cao Mengde [36] wrote in his poem *'On the Longevity of Tortoises and Serpents'*:

> *'Though the divine tortoise lives long,*
>
> *it must one day perish;*
>
> *The soaring serpent may ride the mist,*
>
> *But in the end, it returns to ash.'*

Master Restivo continued, "It implies the ultimate end of every living creature. That is the heart of it."

"As for what will bring about the end of human civilization, this is divine knowledge and should not be taken lightly. For thousands of years, conflicts between civilizations have only grown more intense. Those who understand Heaven's will and act accordingly endure; those who do not are lost.

"In the past century, countless scholars, driven by the rise and fall of dynasties and the waxing and waning of cultures, have tried to find the root cause. Yet even after decades of research, they still haven't found an answer.

"Yet, you disciples have already laid some foundation. If you can dedicate yourselves to sincere inquiry, set aside sectarian pride, and accept wise instruction, you may soon understand the Dharma of Extinction and Stillness."

Monkey-King's Letter to Ivy League School Master

As Master Restivo was speaking, a messenger arrived outside the hall. The mail was from none other than Monkey-King himself.

---

[36] Cao Cao, 曹操 (AD155-220), poet and military ruler in China.

When he left Eastern Land to travel west, he actually wrote to address the challenges of the Ivy League Schools. Which, due to many of his commitments, was mailed a few days ago and had just arrived.

Master Restivo opened the letter and read.

Here are some of the lines from the letter.

"I, the victorious Fighting Buddha Monkey-King, am now visiting America. Your land is beautiful, and I enjoy it a lot.

"I am genuinely seeking cultural exchange and enlightenment. I found a lot of things new to me, and they are fascinating.

"I have observed that the primary trend in our world today is toward unity through diversity, which ultimately leads to harmony, as I hoped. Currently, intermarriage is increasing rapidly, and bloodlines are blending. This has become an unstoppable flow. In three thousand years, all races will merge into one—one skin color, one nation.

"In another eight hundred years, everyone will speak a single language. The conflicts between schools and sects will fade away like smoke in the wind."

"Don't you think so?" The letter concluded.

Master Restivo finished reading and smiled, "Monkey-King is wholly committed to universal harmony. He would lead all beings into the boundless

Nirvana of no remainder—his resolve unshaken, his sincerity true."

"But this Great Harmony he envisions is still far off. Our Western civilization, even though it faces storms now, remains a ship made of sturdy iron and advanced cannons. It still dominates wherever it goes. Assimilation? I don't think we need to worry just yet."

As he spoke, he set the letter aside and closed his eyes in thought.

Suddenly, another messenger showed up, announcing that Old George was coming.

The elder George soon stepped in, smiling proudly. Bowing, he said, "Master, I have gone through many changes since we last met. I now hold a high position, and work keeps me busy day and night. I've missed your teachings—could I trouble you to get some written materials for me to study during my free time?"

Dr. Taylor asked, "And how is your bridge-building project? I heard your racetrack was lost in the fire set by that scoundrel Jenson, and that Monkey-King has gone off to start an insurance company—did you not lose both horse and money?"

George chuckled, "Not at all! Based on Monkey-King's theory of bridge resonance acoustics, I commissioned the development of detection instruments—devices that monitor bridge structures for stress and fractures across the land. We've installed a dozen on every central bridge. They run day and night with superb results. Orders are pouring in from across the globe. Gold flows like water in the Hudson River."

"Only—let none of you tell that Monkey-King! Right now, the U.S. and China are deep in a fierce quarrel over intellectual property rights. Should word get out, it might stir unwanted trouble. We mustn't pour oil on the fire."

Dr. Taylor added with a grin, "Eastern culture does not prize the commodification of knowledge. Years ago, a Chinese physician at our institute taught us acupuncture. He spoke not of patents, but only of friendship—and even, perhaps, of romance."

At this, the assembly burst into hearty laughter.

Master Restivo opened his eye and spoke gravely, "Enough levity. Tell me, where are Monkey-King and Pigsy now? You are all men of letters, yet in your dealings with them these past months, you have gained no advantage, nor much progress."

"Across the American continent today, their names are spoken with reverence: The Eastern Saints! People marvel at the rise of the East, while you still swagger with blind pride.

"I called you all here today for a reason: to get prepared. You need to stand up to them and show them the strength of our Western world. They have 5000 years of history backing them—that ancient rival of ours for centuries. Let's not lose our nerve.

"Cultural exchange starts with conflict—only after clashes does fusion happen. But if we lose now, we might never survive the assimilation."

Adam stepped forward and said, "Monkey-King and Pigsy have generously donated to education and have been named honorary directors at one of our schools. They are visiting today. Because of their large donation, the institution has mobilized everyone to celebrate—and the press has flooded the event."

Master Restivo nodded. "Education is the foundation of culture. Observe, and when the time is right, highlight our system's strengths. If we earn their admiration for our educational methods, it will be a real victory."

Adam added, "That Monkey-King possesses true wisdom and a ready heart. Just days ago, when Asian demon-fish ran rampant in our waters, I told him that Americans love aquatic sports. He immediately suggested the *Aqua-Aerial Fishing Tournament*—a sport blending sky and lakes. Now it's swept across the nation. Every lake has become a battleground for sports. The people are in a frenzy!"

Master Restivo was visibly impressed and said, "To defeat the demon-fish while creating sport, Monkey-King truly gathers and transforms all things. He will surely achieve greatness. You must keep careful watch."

Dr. Taylor bowed and said, "Master, I recently debated Monkey-King on the subject of medicine and healing arts. We fought to a draw, to my disappointment. I have resolved to redouble my study of medical texts and will rechallenge him in the future."

Master Restivo replied, "That match loss is not entirely your fault. The intervention of Guanyin Bodhisattva tipped the balance. Take it seriously; there is still ground to contest in public health, pharmaceutical invention, and anatomical science. Return to your studies and prepare yourself."

Old George now spoke, "I should have beaten that monkey at the racetrack—but Jenson ruined it all. Though I did not win the full contract in bridge bidding, I believe I struck a blow to his momentum. In time, I shall engage him in a battle over the very concept of intellectual property, and show him the marvel of our century-old patent system!"

Master Restivo warned, "Do not take him lightly. You've already made sacrifices when you built that bridge monitor. We are going to duel in other fields; prepare yourself in international relations and military history. I may have you in my other plans."

After a pause, Master Restivo addressed everyone, "This cultural conflict is no minor issue. Monkey-King and Pigsy are no ordinary men. Their arrival in America marks the first time in two thousand years that we meet on equal footing."

When you face them next, take the opportunity to learn. Identify the differences and close the gap between the East and the West. Eastern culture is vast and ancient. Though it may be behind in science, it excels in social governance. Study it thoroughly, and you might discover solutions for many issues in America. Would that not be wonderful?

Cannon Fire and Thunder: Monkey-King Rocks the City

As the disciples prepared to leave, a sudden burst of cannon fire echoed from the riverside. Music blared into the sky. The ground beneath the small riverside town trembled. Everyone exchanged surprised glances.

Messengers raced forward and returned breathlessly, "Monkey-King is touring the nation to award gold medals in the Aqua-Aerial Fishing Championships. Today's ceremony has reached the eastern coast—Boston itself! The whole city has turned out. Crowds fill the streets. Men, women, and children all dressed in their finest, clamoring to witness Monkey-King!"

Master Restivo was surprised. "All this time, we have talked about cultural conflict in vague terms — but Monkey-King has actually stirred the world into action! Since the noise reaches my own doorstep, I must see with my own eyes how Monkey-King rides the winds of fame. Come, everyone — let's go together."

At the riverfront, a large, elevated stage was set up, with colorful flags fluttering in the wind. Music filled the atmosphere. All of Boston's dignitaries had arrived to witness the exciting sports competition. Adam, George, and Taylor led Master Restivo forward and introduced him to Monkey-King. Monkey-King greeted him warmly, and handshakes were exchanged.

Now, dear reader, you might think that Master Restivo—Master of America's scholars—would be seated in the place of honor at the dais. However, after polite greetings, the event staff courteously moved him and his disciples to the rearmost row.

Monkey-King looked around and saw that the front seats were filled with celebrities—film stars, singers, and athletes—who led the crowd in cheers and celebrations. Among them, Pigsy was completely stealing the spotlight.

Monkey-King turned to the organizers and said, "These scholars from Ivy League schools are my honored guests. Might they be invited to sit closer to the front?"

The event organizer, upon hearing Monkey-King's words, hurriedly guided government officials to the back row, trying to lead the Master Restivo delegation to the front. Unexpectedly, Adam stepped in to stop him. He said to Monkey-King, "The public knows nothing of us. The back row is just fine." But Monkey-King was not easily persuaded. Adam sighed and said, "To speak truthfully, this land is not like your Eastern Continent. In the eyes of the common folk here, 'elite intellectuals' like us are held in low regard. Though we are disciples of Master Restivo, we are far from beloved sports stars and movie celebrities." Monkey-King paid no attention, and so the Master Restivo party sat down as he directed.

Master Restivo then said, "Monkey-King, your visit to America was meant to be an earnest exploration of our 'universal values.' Why, then, do you go around showcasing your prowess at every turn, winning admiration but disturbing our order?"

Monkey-King laughed heartily, "I, the Great Sage Equal to Heaven, have never lived by rules or restraints. I act at my pleasure. What is this 'supposed to do' you speak of?"

"While mingling with people, I've felt the differences in customs deeply. As we say, 'when you travel, you experience a change of dialect every ten miles, for custom it will differ every hundred.' Now separated by oceans and continents, do you truly expect to find one 'universal value' that fits all?"

Master Restivo responded sternly, "I've heard many of your brash ways—today I see them firsthand. But I ask you this: the exchange of cultures between East and West is now a global tide. True exchange must flow both ways. I plan to take my students to your land—will you support this effort? I've heard that your continent remains a backwater, closed off and uninformed, and full of inconveniences."

At this, Monkey-King burst out laughing, "It is the Americans who live in ignorance! Our people know your ways in every detail, while yours are completely unaware of ours. Next year, I will host a grand cultural exchange summit atop Flower-Fruit Mountain. Come, and see for yourself!"

Adam said, "You are right. We have been blind for too long. But how can Americans understand your Divine Continent when American media bias blinds them? They ignore our virtues and focus on sensational news, disasters, and misfortune. Why not let Pigsy expand his martial arts academy, develop tourism in your land, and promote cultural exchange—so our people can see the East with their own eyes?"

Pigsy hurriedly protested, "I work day and night, where would I find the time? Let Monkey Brother handle it—he lives free as a cloud!"

Charles River Celebration — Fishing, Festivities

Let's return to the scene by the Charles River. Right now, boats race side by side, and startled fish leap into the air in sparkling arcs. Water splashes like stars as strong young men and women sit in the boats, quick-eyed and sure-handed, catching fish in large numbers. Some fall into the water, blurring the line between man and fish, as the crowd cheers for miles downriver. Flags flutter; joy rises—a festive scene!

Below the awards platform, participants arrived in waves, unloading fish from their vehicles into a line of large machines. The machine chimed melodiously, weighing each catch, and with a sharp clang, filleted fish neatly rolled into bags. People eagerly scooped them up, praising the sport as a marvel—cleaning the environment while feeding the people.

The event organizer came to invite Monkey-King to present the awards. Monkey-King handed out gold and silver medals to each winner as the national anthem played, eliciting thunderous applause.

Just then, a few business elites approached Pigsy, "This fishing sport has become increasingly popular and trendy, but the demon-fish are nearly gone. We suggest breeding them in controlled waters—may we count on your support, Master?"

Pigsy frowned, "The last time I released fish into the wild, I was nearly sued. Why would I repeat such folly?"

"Not to worry," said the businessman. "I've already secured permits from the state. When the officials heard about the profits to be made, they dared not say no. The rest—I'll share in confidence another day." Everyone laughed heartily.

A Tidal Shift: From Celebration to Political Change

Let's not dwell on how these merchants flattered Pigsy or how he eventually agreed. Master Restivo, noticing how Monkey-King and Pigsy mingled with both the people and officials like old friends, turned to his disciples and said, "The masses love these two Chinese. We are utterly eclipsed. If Monkey-King can come to our land and stir such waves, we too must journey to his East Divine Continent and see it for ourselves."

His disciples all agreed, "We shall draft our plans immediately. We will study abroad in China! We will not let our master down!"

As they spoke, a storm of applause broke out. On stage, a government official gave an energetic speech, urging the cultivation of Asian carp and the expansion of the aquatic sports movement. He pledged to create thousands of jobs and announced the construction of Eastern Plaza, a hub for cultural exchange, trade, and tourism. The crowd whistled, and a cheer rose.

But then, he added confidently, "I am a man of quick action. Tomorrow I will appoint a director, and billions will be invested. I will not let the people rejoice in vain! We will find the right person for the new prestigious job."

Yet even before he finished, murmurs swelled through the crowd—then grew into a rhythmic chant:

"Monkey-King! Pigsy! Monkey-King! Pigsy!"

The waves of voices rolled like thunder.

Seeing the official frozen on stage, his aide whispered urgently. It turned out that the people had chosen Monkey-King and Pigsy to lead the Eastern Plaza project themselves. The will of the masses was unstoppable.

The official, always mindful of public opinion, quickly signaled for Monkey-King and Pigsy to step forward and announced their appointments. Master Restivo, along with Adam, George, and Taylor, moved forward to congratulate them. Cheers and applause erupted in a thunderous roar that shook the heavens.

Figure 22 "Good, Great Sage!" And true to his nature, Monkey-King acted at once. With a single somersault, he soared into the clouds, brandishing his golden staff, light radiating in all directions. Gazing afar at the splendid mountains and rivers of America, he danced through the sky, scattering clusters of white clouds in his wake. When the clouds drifted away, a modern plaza by the riverside, pointed spires, and domed rooftops appeared under the blue sky.

Monkey-King Ascends through Clouds — A New Era of Cultural Exchanges

Now Wukong, true to his name as Monkey-King, didn't delay. One somersault launched him into the clouds. With a golden pole spinning, light shoots in all directions. From above, he gazed upon the beautiful American landscape. Wherever he danced, white clouds streamed forth. When the clouds dispersed, a gleaming modern plaza by the river appeared beneath the blue sky—spires, domes, and towers in futuristic style; below, the busy crowds celebrated.

Dear readers, don't underestimate this Eastern Plaza! This isn't just a building—it's the beginning of a new era of cultural exchange. As the tides of the 21st century rise, East and West will meet, not in conflict but in mutual understanding.

A Verse to Mark the Moment

Across four continents for eight thousand years,
We've witnessed rises, falls, and countless tears.
When desert winds blow, only ruins remain,
No crowds, no nations, just time's silent reign.

East and West now duel with strength and might,
Each holds its glory, each claims its right.
Look upon this small blue globe in the endless skies,
Heaven and earth, sun and moon—differences die.

Alas, my readers, this is the true adventurous tale of Wukong, the Monkey King, in America. So be it.

www.ingramcontent.com/pod-product-compliance
Lightning Source LLC
Chambersburg PA
CBHW022149170626
46807CB00005B/2134